AN
ORCA
YOUNG
READER

Road Trip

ERIC WALTERS

ORCA BOOK PUBLISHERS

National Library of Canada cataloguing in publication data
Walters, Eric, 1957–
Road trip

(An Orca young reader)

IBSN 1-55143-201-3

I. Title. PS8595.A598R62 2002   jC813'.54   C2002-910199-9

PZ7.W17129Ro 2002

Library of Congress Catalog Card Number: 2002101604

Orca Book Publishers gratefully acknowledges the support of its publishing programs provided by the following agencies: the Department of Canadian Heritage, the Canada Council for the Arts, and the British Columbia Arts Council.

Cover design by Christine Toller
Cover and interior illustrations by John Mantha
Printed and bound in Canada

IN CANADA	IN THE UNITED STATES
Orca Book Publishers	Orca Book Publishers
PO Box 5626, Station B	PO Box 468
Victoria, BC Canada	Custer, WA USA
V8R 6S4	98240-0468

04 • 5 4 3 2

For all the people who give their time and energy to help make children's sports happen.

E.W.

Collect all of Eric Walters' basketball books featuring Nick and Kia:

\# 1 - *Three on Three*

\# 2 - *Full Court Press*

\# 3 - *Hoop Crazy*

\# 4 - *Long Shot*

\# 5 - *Road Trip*

Other books by Eric Walters, for older readers:

War of the Eagles

Caged Eagles

Chapter One

"It's pretty strange having my two guys going away without me," my mother said as she leaned in the open sliding door of the van.

"I guess it is a little different," I admitted.

Mom always had gone with us when we went away for basketball tournaments. Actually, we always went everywhere as a family.

"At least I'll be able to get a lot of work done without you and your dad around here to distract me."

"That's a big plus," I agreed. "Besides, it isn't like we'll be gone that long. We'll be back in two days. Sooner if we lose our first games."

"I'll miss you, but in that case I'm hoping I

won't be seeing you until very, very late Sunday night," she said as she leaned farther in and ruffled my hair. "Either way, though, remember this is supposed to be about having fun more than it is about winning."

"I know."

"I know *you* know, let's just hope your father and your coach remember that."

"It will be fun," I reassured her. "Dad said it'll be just a bunch of guys having fun."

"Hey, do I look like a guy?" Kia questioned from the seat in the back corner.

"Okay," I admitted as I turned around. "A bunch of guys and one girl."

"That's better," she huffed.

Mom flashed a big smile at Kia. "At least with you going along we know there's one responsible person to take care of everything."

"Are you saying that Dad and Coach aren't responsible?" I asked.

She smirked, and didn't answer.

"This was certainly an *interesting* idea your coach had to exclude the parents from this trip," my mother said.

Interesting is one of those words that means that you don't necessarily agree with something or think that it's right.

We were going far away to compete in a tournament to start our year. It was a big tournament

— one of the biggest tournaments anywhere. And the only parent going along, besides the coach himself, was my parent. My dad was sort of the unofficial assistant coach. Besides, Coach needed a second person to drive half the team.

"And why exactly did your coach think this was such a good idea?" Mom questioned.

"He said if we're going to bond as a team that a trip like this is important," I explained.

We'd been together for only a few weeks, and half of the team were new guys. Coach thought it was important for us to become one team and not six new players and six players from last year's team.

"Bonding I understand, but why no parents?" my mother asked.

"He didn't want there to be any distractions."

"Silly me," she said. "All this time I thought I was your mother, and now I find out I'm a distraction."

"Come on, Mom, don't be like that. Coach knows about how important it is for us to become a team," I said, defending his decision.

A look of doubt crossed her face for a split second and then vanished. "I'm sure he does."

"Just think of all the championship teams he played on," Kia added.

There was no denying any of that. Coach Barkley was practically a basketball legend from his days playing high school and college ball. He'd even played parts of two seasons in the NBA before injuries forced him to retire.

Of course, this was the first time he'd ever tried to be a coach. His son, L.B., was part of the team and that was a big part of why he volunteered to coach. Nobody could argue with how much he knew about basketball, but there were some big problems — problems that almost caused the team to end before it even began.

Coach Barkley seemed to know everything about basketball and coaching it, but hadn't known much about coaching nine-year-old kids. He was really trying now to be more relaxed and not take things so seriously. There were still times, though, that I could see things bubbling under the surface. I was pretty sure my mother could see it too, and that was why she was anxious about not going along on this first tournament.

"Besides, Dad will be there to help take care of everything," I offered, trying to read her mind.

"You're right," she admitted. "Although trusting your dad to be a calm, quiet and reasonable person in the heat of a basketball game is a bit of a stretch."

"Dad's very responsible!" I protested.

Mom huffed. "He's responsible everywhere in the world . . . except for the sidelines of a basketball game."

That was another one of those points that was hard to argue. Something about the game often brought out another side in him.

"Speaking of your father, where is he?" my mother asked.

Almost like magic he came out of the front door. In his hand was a small overnight bag that held all the things he'd need for the next two nights. He opened the door and plopped behind the wheel, dropping the bag on the floor beside him.

"Okay, you've got the number at the hotel where we're staying, right?" he asked my mother.

"Written down on the calendar," my mother answered.

"I guess we better get going," my father said. "We still have four more kids to pick up."

"Are you all sure that you have everything?" my mother asked.

All three of us nodded our heads and mumbled that we were all set.

"And Nick, do you have *everything*?" she asked me.

I could tell by the tone of her voice and the look on her face that she was doing more than asking me a question. I did a quick mental check – toothbrush, basketball shoes, CD player, underwear, bathing suit, extra shorts, basketball uniform. I was positive. I'd been extra careful. I could picture me putting all of them into my bag and . . .

It was then that I saw that my mother was holding my bag.

"You left it on the bench in the entranceway," she explained as she handed it to me.

I took the bag and quickly put it behind the third seat.

"You're going to have to take care of your own things," my father said sternly. "Your mother isn't going to be there to take care of her little boy this weekend."

I nodded my head.

"What if we didn't notice you didn't have your bag until we got to the hotel?" he asked. "It isn't like we could drive seven hours each way to get it. It's a long drive."

"Speaking of which – not that I want to get rid of you – but you better get going," my mother said.

She climbed slightly into the van and wrapped her arms around me.

"Be good, be safe, and help take care of each other," she said as she kissed me on the cheek.

"We'll be okay, Mom, don't worry."

She gave me one more squeeze, then released her grip, retreated from the van and slammed the door closed. She then circled around to the other side, leaned in the driver's window and gave my father a hug and a kiss.

"You be sure to call as soon as you check in," she said. "Promise?"

"I don't like making promises that I can't keep," my father said. "You know how I sometimes forget."

"I'll worry until I hear from you."

"We'll really try to remember," my father offered.

"Please do more than *try*!"

"Don't worry, I'll remind them," Kia offered.

My mother gave Kia another big smile. I would have said something in protest, but it was more likely that it would be Kia who remembered than either my father or me.

"Now you really better get going," my mother said.

My father nodded his head in agreement, but instead of going he fumbled around in his seat.

"What's wrong?" my mother asked.

"We can't go."

"Why not?" she asked.

"I forgot my keys," my father said sheepishly. He jumped out of the van and ran up the path of the house.

My mother leaned into the van one more time. "Kia," she said. "I'm counting on you."

Kia just smiled in reply.

Chapter Two

My father looked at his watch and then checked the time against the clock on the dashboard. There was a one-minute difference between the two, but both indicated that we were a tiny bit early. It was two minutes before eight, the time we were supposed to meet Coach Barkley and the rest of the team.

All the time we'd been driving around picking up the other guys I could tell that my father was anxious about us being late. He hadn't said anything, but I knew by the frequent glances at his watch and the way he was driving just a little faster than usual. I had to agree that it probably was important to be on time.

Coach Barkley was a fanatic about being on time.

Practices started and ended right on schedule. Anybody who wasn't there on the dot could count on having to run a dozen extra laps. Even worse, if you weren't there thirty minutes early before a game – even an exhibition game – you'd be watching the whole first half from the end of the bench.

"I wonder where your coach is?" my father asked.

"Technically he's not late yet," I pointed out.

"But he's always early," my father said.

He was right about that. It seemed that no matter how early we got to a game or practice he was already there. I once asked L.B., his son, about how early they arrived. He just shook his head and told me I wouldn't believe him if he told me.

"Maybe somebody wasn't ready," Kia piped in from the back seat.

"Maybe *Coach* wasn't ready," Tristan added.

There were a few seconds of quiet and then everybody broke up laughing.

There were now seven of us in the van. Along with me, my father and Kia, we'd picked up Jamie, Mark, Tristan and David. This was the third year the six of us had been together on the same team, and after that length of time you've gotten to know each other pretty well. I guess the real important part of this trip was for us to get to know the other six players just as well.

"Maybe while we're waiting we better set down some ground rules," my father said as he turned around in his seat.

"What do you mean ground rules?" I asked.

"Rules for the drive."

"Rules? How complicated can it be?" I asked. "You drive, we sit."

"It's a little more complicated than that."

"How much more complicated can it be?" I questioned.

"It's a long trip, so we need some rules so we don't drive each other crazy," my father explained.

"We won't drive each other crazy," I argued.

"Okay, so we need rules so you all don't drive *me* crazy," my father said. "Remember, this is a very long drive."

"How long is it?" Tristan asked.

"If we drive straight through it's about seven hours, so when you throw in food, getting gas and washroom breaks, it's probably going to take us closer to nine hours."

"Nine hours!" Tristan exclaimed. "So that means we're not going to get there until, like, five o'clock."

"That's if everything goes right, and that's why we need to establish those rules."

"What did you have in mind?" I asked.

"Some basic things," my father replied. "Stay

in your seats, don't throw things around the van, try not to spill food or drinks, pass your garbage forward to go into the garbage bag. And, most important, the first person to ask 'are we there yet' or to start singing about bottles of beer on the wall will be walking! Everybody understand?"

"Understood," I said as everybody else mumbled agreement and nodded their heads.

"Good, because it looks like we're just about ready to get started," my father said as Coach Barkley's vehicle pulled in just in front of us.

It came to a stop and the coach got out and walked back toward our van. He leaned in the open window of the driver's door.

"Any problems?" he asked my father.

"None. You?"

"Not much. Sorry we're a bit late. I had to double back because one of the guys forgot his bag."

Kia burst out laughing. She was the only one other than my father who knew about me almost forgetting my bag.

"I asked L.B. twice if he'd packed everything, and he had, except he forgot to put the bag in the car. Can you believe that?"

I could see the start of a smirk on my father's face in the reflection in the rearview mirror. Was he going to say something about me doing the same thing?

11

"The important thing is that he's got it now," my father said. "People forget things."

Coach Barkley leaned even farther into the van. "Does everybody *here* have their bags?"

There were a few chuckles and everybody agreed they had their stuff stowed in the back.

"In that case we should hit the road. How about I lead and you follow for the first while?" Coach Barkley suggested.

"Works for me," my father replied. "I was thinking we could go until around noon or even one and have a late lunch."

"Sounds good."

My father started the van as the coach walked back toward his vehicle.

"Here we go. The first step to winning a tournament is getting there."

The first thirty minutes or so hadn't been so bad. Then it started to drag more and more, and now it felt like even the van was moving slower. Maybe it wouldn't have been so bad if the batteries in my CD player hadn't died. I had some extras in my bag – buried at the back beneath everybody else's bags – but I really couldn't get those until we stopped. How long would that be?

I looked at the dashboard clock – two whole minutes had passed since the last time I had looked.

That meant we were now two hours *and* two minutes into the trip – which of course meant we only had six hours and fifty-eight minutes to go.

"Dad?" I called out. "How long before — "

"Ground rules!" he barked at me. "Don't forget the ground rules!"

"I wasn't asking about how much longer the trip is," I explained.

"But if somebody was to ask," Tristan piped in from the back, "just suppose they were . . . what would the answer be?"

"Six hours and fifty-eight . . . no, make that fifty-seven minutes," I answered before my father could cut me off.

"Come on, that can't be right," Kia argued. "We've already been in this van forever."

"It just *seems* like forever. Actually, it's only been two hours and three minutes," I said.

"Nope, has to be longer," Jamie argued.

"Stop it!" my father bellowed. "Just stop it! I'm not going to listen to the six of you complain about the drive for the next seven hours!"

"Seven hours! I thought it was only six!" Tristan protested.

"It is six hours *and* fifty-seven minutes," I said.

"No, it's less!" Kia yelled. "Look, the clock just changed! It's only six hours and fifty-six minutes!"

A cheer went up and filled the van with noise.

"Everybody quiet down!" my father yelled, and the van fell silent.

"I think that it might be good — for everybody, if we took a short break."

Chapter Three

My father eased the van into the exit lane and we slowed down, finally pulling into an empty parking spot right in front of the service center. Coach Barkley and the rest of the guys pulled in two spaces over.

"Everybody stick together and remember this is only a short stop!" my father shouted as the doors popped open.

I climbed out and stretched. It felt good to unfold my legs and body.

Coach Barkley and the rest of the team walked over and joined the seven of us. We all strolled toward the door.

"Stopping was a good idea," the coach said. "These guys were just starting to drive me a little crazy. How come you got all the quiet ones?"

"Me?" my father protested. "I thought you had the better part of this deal!"

"Not me. I'd trade you kids for the next part of the trip."

"Now that's a deal!" my father exclaimed.

"Don't we have any say in that?" I questioned.

The coach cocked an eye at me. "What's wrong, Nick, don't you trust my driving?"

"No, I trust your driving."

"Then it has to be my company. Is that what it is?"

"No, no! Of course not!" I protested.

Coach started to laugh. "Good, then it's settled. You'll be in my van for the next part of the drive."

I was the last to get into the van, which explained why I was sitting in the front seat, right beside Coach. As I turned around to face the guys I could see the smirk on Kia's face.

"Does anybody mind if I put on a little music?" Coach Barkley asked.

"No . . . of course not," I said, and the others voiced agreement. My CD player and headset were in my father's van.

"I always find it makes the time go a little bit faster if you have good music playing," Coach Barkley said.

"Music is great . . . depending on what sort of music," Kia piped in from the back.

"How about if I let you choose?" Coach Barkley offered.

"We can put on any CD we want?" David asked.

"I was thinking about any of *my* CDs," Coach Barkley said.

I had a sinking feeling. The coach and my father were always exchanging CDs so I knew what sort of music we could expect.

"I think I'd rather we just drove without music," I suggested.

"Are you sure that's such a good idea?" Coach asked. "Music relaxes me, and when I'm relaxed I'm much, *much* easier to be around."

"All in favor of music raise your hand!" Tristan said loudly from the very back corner.

Six hands shot up in the air.

"That's more like it," Coach Barkley said. "Go ahead, Nick, look through my CD case and make a choice."

I reached down and unzipped the case. There had to be two dozen CDs. I started to scan the covers. Grover Washington Jr., Dave Koz, Miles Davis, George Benson, Warren Hill . . . I knew them all. Every single one of them. Nothing but jazz.

"Bet you recognize some of them from your father's music collection," Coach Barkley said.

17

"Not some of them. All of them."

"Good, then you can select the one that the guys will like the best."

I looked over my shoulder at the guys. "Anybody have any *favorite* jazz performers?"

There was a stunned silence, almost immediately followed by some chuckling.

"What's wrong, don't people like jazz?" Coach asked.

"It wouldn't be my first choice," Kia answered.

"And what would be your first choice?" Coach asked. "One of those loud rap songs, or hop hip music?"

"That's hip hop," Jamie said, correcting him.

Whatever it's called, it's hardly music. Do you know where I first learned to appreciate jazz?"

"Where?" I asked.

"In the locker rooms when I was in the bigs," Coach said.

"The bigs?" David asked.

"The pros," Jamie explained.

"When our team was on the road, the guys would always spend time in jazz clubs. Kansas, L.A., Detroit, Boston and of course New York – you name a city, and I've heard jazz there."

"Pro basketball players like jazz?" Kia asked, sounding amazed. "I'm positive they like rap and hip hop and reggae."

"Maybe now, but not before," Coach explained.

"It's really all the same, you know," Tristan said.

"It is?" a number of people asked at once.

"How do you figure that?" Coach asked.

"I was watching this TV show and it said that jazz music is sort of the great-grandfather of rap music."

"That's a scary thought," Coach said. "Throw on something, Nick."

I scanned the case again. It really didn't matter much what I chose.

"Music makes the time pass more quickly," Coach said. "We still have a long drive ahead of us."

"Coach, why did you want us to come to this tournament?" Tristan asked. "There have to be closer ones we could have gone to."

"No question about that, but there are a lot of teams traveling a lot farther than we are," Coach said.

"Farther than a nine-hour drive?" I asked in amazement.

"Some of them will be driving for two or three days while others are taking a nine-hour *plane* ride."

"Nine-hour plane ride? In nine hours you could fly right across the whole country!"

"Farther than that. This is an international tournament. There're the best teams from Canada and the United States, but there're also going to be teams from Mexico and Europe."

"People are flying there from Europe to play in a basketball tournament?" Kia questioned.

"Not just a basketball tournament, but *the* basketball tournament. This one is special."

"But what makes it so special?" David asked.

"The teams that will be there. Most tournaments are open to any team that applies, but not this one."

"You need an invitation, right?" I said.

"That's right. Any team is free to apply, but the organizers decide who's good enough to get an invitation. Hundreds of teams apply, and then they select only the top forty teams."

"There's going to be forty teams?" I questioned in amazement. "That's gigantic!"

"It's hard to narrow it down any farther. The forty best teams."

"And that's who we're going to be playing against?" I asked.

"Every single game is going to be tough. Probably the best team you played all of last season is only as good as the bottom teams in this tournament."

I thought about that for a second and decided I really didn't want to think about it any more. It wasn't like we'd won every game last year.

"But just how do they even know which teams

are good enough and which aren't?" Kia asked.

"There's a whole committee that makes that decision. The committee is made up of basketball experts from around the country."

"Experts? What sort of experts?" I asked.

"College and high school coaches, scouts and former professional players," Coach explained.

"Still, even if they know basketball, how do they know which teams are the best? It isn't like they've seen us play," Kia persisted.

"Along with our application I had to submit your schedule and record for last year," Coach explained.

"And our record was good enough?" I asked. "We were one of the forty best teams?"

"We must be, 'cause they let us in," Tristan said from the back.

"Your record was pretty good, but I had to make a few calls as well," Coach said.

"Calls to who?" I asked.

"I still have some basketball contacts. I know a couple of the guys on the selection committee. I told them about the team and they agreed we deserved an invitation."

"That's good," I said, although I wasn't that convinced. That meant that maybe we weren't even good enough to be here in the first place but the Coach talked them into letting us in anyway.

"It'll be exciting, but for me it'll be a walk

down memory lane," Coach said.

"You've been here before?" I asked.

"I was here with my rep team when I was your age."

"Wow, so this tournament has been going on practically forever," Kia said.

"Watch it, Kia! I'm not quite that old. It was only thirty-four years ago."

"Thirty-four years? That sounds like forever to me," Tristan replied. "So how did your team do?"

"We did all right," Coach said quietly.

"All right like you won a couple of games, or all right like you won the whole tournament?" Tristan asked.

Coach smiled and looked back over his shoulder. "What do you think?"

"I think you aced the whole thing and walked away with the first-place trophy," Tristan replied.

Coach smiled again.

"Well?" Kia asked. "Is he right?"

"Tristan is half right. We did walk away with a trophy – second place. We lost in the finals."

"That's still pretty good," I offered.

"Losing in the finals is still losing. I played terribly . . . I let things get to me. I let the size of the crowd distract me."

"There was a big crowd?" Kia asked.

"The biggest I ever played in front of until I

got to university."

"How big was it?" I asked.

"Over six thousand people."

A rumble of response spread around the van. The largest crowd I'd ever played for was about two hundred at most.

"And we'll be playing in front of a crowd that big?" I demanded.

"Only if we get as far as the finals."

"Do you think we can do that?" Jamie asked. "Get to the finals?"

"These teams are the very best around."

"And we were one of the best teams in our division last year," Tristan said.

"You played well. You were a good team last year, and you're better now than you were then. But this isn't just your division. These are the best teams from the top divisions everywhere," Coach said.

"So you don't think we can do it?" I asked.

"I'm not saying that."

"So you think we *can* win it all?" Tristan asked.

"I'm not saying that either. I'm a coach, not a fortuneteller. All I can tell you for sure is that right now, before the tournament starts, you have the same record as every other team and the same chance of winning as anybody else . . . that is, if you want it."

Everybody screamed out how much they wanted

it. I wanted it too . . . but every single player coming to this tournament wanted to win. The question in my mind wasn't if we wanted it, but if we were good enough.

"So, Nick, are you going to give me a CD or aren't you?" Coach asked.

"Sure . . . yeah . . . of course," I said as I startled out of my thoughts and handed him a CD.

He clicked it in place and the saxophone of Grover Washington Jr. started coming out of the speakers. I didn't think that this music would make the trip seem any shorter – it would just make me *want* it to be shorter.

Chapter Four

"Wake up, Nick, we're here!"

"Where?" I asked, rubbing my eyes.

"The hotel . . . the resort . . . we've arrived," my father replied.

"How long was I asleep?" I asked.

"Close to three hours."

Right after lunch we'd changed back to our original vehicles. I'd clipped on my headset, my CD player now equipped with new batteries, closed my eyes and gone to sleep.

My father slowed down as we drove down the long driveway. On both sides were large, lush lawns, and flower beds, and tennis courts. Off to the right there was a swimming pool. At one end of the pool was a high, high tower and diving board. It looked awfully high. There was no way I was going off that tower, but I planned to spend a whole lot of time around the pool. One of the very best things about going away for a tournament was being around the pool and everybody just fooling around and having a great time.

"Look at the sign!" Kia said, pointing ahead.

There in gigantic letters it said "Welcome Basketball Players! Tournament Headquarters!"

"Len said that almost all the teams are staying right here at the resort," my father said.

He pulled the van to a stop right under the overhang in front of the main entrance. I looked back to see Coach Barkley pull in right behind us.

"Everybody out," my father announced. "And make sure you take your bags and things with you."

We all tumbled out of the van and circled around to the back of the vehicle. My father opened the doors and bags started to tumble out. He stopped them with his body and then started to pass out everybody's bag.

"Anybody want to go for a swim?" Kia asked.

"No swimming," my father said. "Everybody needs to get their stuff up to their room and get settled in before *anybody* goes *anywhere*."

"Here we are, all safe and sound!" Coach Barkley said as he came up beside us along with the

other half of the team.

"That was some drive," my father said.

"Not too bad. As soon as we get everybody checked in, I want to have a team meeting in my room," Coach said.

"Sounds good . . . see you up there in ten minutes."

"Here we are," my father said as he swiped the card against the door and the little light turned green. He pushed open the door of our room.

"We're all staying in the same room?" Tristan asked as he pushed in right behind my father.

"Seven of us are staying in the same *double* room," my father explained as we all crowded into the room. "And Coach Barkley and the other six guys are staying in a double room across the hall."

The room had two double beds, a big dresser with a large TV atop it, and sliding doors opening up to a balcony.

"The other room is right through this door," my father said as he pushed it open. We all surged through after him, although there really wasn't anything new or different to see – the second room was identical.

"So who sleeps where?" David asked.

"You, Jamie, Tristan and Mark sleep in this

room — two of you in each bed — and Nick, Kia and I get the other room. Nick shares with me and Kia, of course, gets her own bed," my father explained.

"You see? There are some advantages to being a girl," Kia said. "Although that advantage isn't as big as you'd think, because I have to share a room with Nick."

"What's wrong with being in my room?" I demanded.

"Are you kidding? It's like sleeping with a chain saw running in the same room!"

"It's not that bad!" I protested. Besides, what did she have to complain about? I was the one who had to share a bed with my father. What Kia didn't know was that my mother always said that compared to my father I didn't make a sound.

"At least we won't hear him from the other room," Tristan said. "We'll close the door and — "

"The door isn't ever going to be closed," my father said, cutting him off. "My job is to watch all of you, and I can't supervise through a closed door."

"Okay," Tristan said. "So the door stays open."

"And nobody goes in or out through the hall door in your room. The door to the hall from your room stays closed, locked and chained. Everybody goes in and out through the door in my room. Any questions?"

"None," Tristan said, holding up his hands.

"Sounds okay to me," Jamie agreed.

"Then let's drop our bags and meet with the coach," my father said.

"Sounds good," Kia agreed. "The sooner we start the meeting, the sooner we end the meeting, and the sooner we can get into the pool!"

I went back into the first room along with Kia and my father. I dropped my bag at the foot of one of the beds.

"Not that one," my father said. "The one closest to the door."

"But this one's closer to the TV!" I protested.

"You can see the TV just fine from this one. I have to be by the door to better watch things," he said.

"What do you think we're going to do, make a break for it when you're sleeping?" I demanded.

"I don't think you're going to do anything. My job is to take care of things and this is the best place to keep my eye on everything. Any more questions and you'll be sleeping in the closet."

"Fine . . . whatever," I mumbled as I moved my bag over. There was no sense in arguing.

"Hurry up, guys!" my father yelled through the door into the other room. He then opened the door to the hall in time to see the last of the others heading into the room directly across the hall.

Everybody scrambled to the door after him and we rushed through, following right behind the rest of the team into their rooms across the hall.

"Four of you drop your bags in the other room," Coach bellowed. "Two of you get one of the beds in this room, and I get my own bed."

Quickly they all sorted themselves out, and everybody assembled in the one room.

"Now that we're here let's get a few things straight," Coach said. "First thing, did anybody come here, drive all that way, because they wanted to lose?"

"I don't ever want to lose nothing," Tristan said.

There was no arguing that. Tristan was a great guy, but he played every game – and every practice – like his life depended on it. That was great during the games when he was on our side, but if you were playing against him in practice, he brought new meaning to the term "hard foul."

"Is Tristan the only one?" Coach demanded.

"No, of course not!" Kia argued. "We came to win!"

"All of us," Jamie agreed.

"No losers here," I added.

Coach nodded. "Good . . . that's the place to start. If you think the drive here was long, think about how much longer it'll be if we go home

31

without playing to our potential."

If we didn't do well, I was going to make super sure that I wasn't sharing the ride with the coach — or, for that matter, sitting up front beside my father. Back corner, farthest from either driver, would be the prime piece of real estate.

"I want you all to remember that winning or losing doesn't start on the court with the jump ball. It starts right now. Do you know what lots of the other teams are going to be doing tonight?"

"Sleeping?" Kia questioned.

"The smart ones. Other teams are going to be out playing miniature golf, or rock climbing, or eating big meals or doing other foolish things."

"Like swimming?" Kia asked hesitantly.

"Yeah, like swimming," Coach agreed. "Do you know that swimming takes away muscle strength and makes you sluggish? Swimming is the last thing in the world that any of us are going to be doing."

"You mean we can't swim at all?" Kia asked.

"No swimming."

"Not at all?" David asked. "Even a little?"

"Well . . . maybe if there's enough time between games you can all go into the pool to cool off, but nobody swims."

"What are we supposed to do in a pool if we can't swim?" Tristan asked.

"You can jump in, get cool, but no swimming."

"Could we go in tonight?" Kia asked. "We don't have a game until tomorrow."

"I'm afraid there isn't enough time. By the time the reception is over, it'll be close to nine o'clock."

"But then we'll still have time to go for a swim," Kia said.

"Afraid not. I want everybody back in their rooms, lights out, by nine-thirty," Coach said.

"Nine-thirty!" half a dozen voices called out.

"That's what I said. We're going to be one of the smart teams. We'll be sleeping while some of the other teams are swimming, or watching movies, or eating junk food, or running around the hotel."

Or doing one of dozens of other things that would be fun.

"Two more things," Coach Barkley said. "Nobody, and I repeat, nobody, goes anywhere by themselves, and you don't go anywhere no matter how many of you there are unless you clear it with either myself or Nick's dad."

"Does everybody understand that?" my father asked. "We're responsible for you, and we can't be responsible if we don't know where you are at all times."

"And the last thing I want to warn you about is that I don't want any of you talking to the press unless one of us is around."

"Talking to the press?" I asked. "You mean, like, reporters?"

"Newspaper and TV people," Coach said.

"There's going to be TV people here?" Tristan asked in amazement.

"You're joking, right?" I asked.

"No joke."

"And they're here to cover the games we're playing?" I asked.

"I told you all how big this tournament is. This is one of the biggest events this town has all year. There'll be reporters there tonight at the reception, and you can bet we're going to attract a certain amount of their attention," Coach said.

"We are?" David asked.

"I played my college ball just down the road from here," Coach explained.

"And people still remember from so long ago?" Tristan asked.

Coach shot Tristan a dirty look. "More than you'd believe. But besides that, we're a little different than the other teams."

"How are we different?" Kia asked.

"Because of you."

"Me?"

"There are forty teams here, and each team has twelve players. That makes a total of four hundred and eighty players. Do you know how many of them are girls?"

I was pretty sure I already knew the answer to that question.

"One?" she asked.

"And, you are not simply the only female ballplayer this year. In the entire thirty-seven-year history of this tournament, you are only the second female participant."

"That's hard to believe," Kia said.

Coach shook his head. "But true. And that first player was here thirty-four years ago."

"Isn't that when you were here as a kid?" I asked, remembering what he'd told us during the ride.

"That's right," Coach said. "That was the tournament where I was a player."

"And did you play against her?" Jamie asked.

"Not against her," he said with a smile.

"It was your sister, wasn't it?" I said. "And she was on your team."

"That's right. My sister, Chris, was on my team."

Coach had a twin sister, and I remembered he'd told me that when they were kids they always played on the same team. She was supposed to be really good.

"So, Kia, since you're the only girl here, there's going to be a lot of eyes staring in your direction."

"So what else is new?" Kia asked.

Kia was right — what was different about that? Kia was pretty well always the only girl whether it was on the rep team or the school team or when we played in three-on-three contests. And somehow she hardly ever let any of it bother her. She just went out and played her game.

I knew I could never have handled it that well. I always felt nervous before any game. But not Kia. She always acted calm, and cool, and confident. Sometimes I knew that was just an act, but it was such a good act that she had everybody else fooled. Not me, though. I could tell when she was upset or scared. You spend all of your time with somebody and you get to see what nobody else sees.

Of course, that also meant that Kia knew me. Sometimes it felt like she could read my mind, and sometimes I didn't want anybody – even my best friend – to be doing that.

"So if there are no more questions, I want you all to get dressed for the reception," Coach said.

Coach had insisted that each one of us pack dress clothes for the reception. He said a team has to look like a team even when they aren't on the court. Of all the things Coach had said that my mother questioned, this one instruction she completely agreed with. She thought we'd look so "cute" all dressed up.

"I still think a T-shirt and sneakers would be the right way to dress for a basketball reception," Kia said.

The coach cast an angry eye at her. "You did bring dress clothes, didn't you?"

Kia gave a disgusted look. "My mother said she packed them for me."

"Good. Everybody has to be dressed and in the hall in five minutes."

Chapter Five

"Hurry up!" my father bellowed into the next room as he struggled with his tie.

My mother usually did his ties for him, and he didn't seem to be doing very well. He'd tied and untied it two times already. First it was too short, and then too long.

I loosened the loop in mine — my mother had tied it for me the night before — and then slipped it over my head and around my neck. The tie, combined with a long-sleeved white shirt with a collar, black dress pants and black leather shoes, made it feel like I was heading to church.

"Come on, guys!" my father yelled again. He stood before the mirror making the final adjustments to his tie, now satisfied that it was the right length.

David, followed by Jamie and then Mark, came into the room. They all looked equally dressy and equally uncomfortable. The only noticeable difference was that David was wearing one of his shiny black dress shoes and holding the second in his hands.

"Those things both go on your feet, you know," my father said to David.

"I can't get it on," he said. "It doesn't fit."

"Didn't you try them on before you packed them?" my father asked.

"I wore them to church last month, but I think my feet have grown since then."

"Come on, your feet couldn't have grown since . . . " My father let the sentence trail off because he realized that David *could* have grown since then. I knew that I kept outgrowing my shoes before I ever had a chance to wear them out.

"How could only one foot grow?" Jamie asked.

"Most people have one foot slightly bigger than the other. Have a seat here," my father said, patting the bed, "and I'll try to get your shoe on."

David sat down and my father took the shoe from him.

"Point your toe and take a deep breath," my father said.

"A deep breath?" Jamie questioned.

"It can't hurt," my father said with a shrug.

He put the shoe on David's foot and wiggled it around as David grunted and groaned.

"Press harder!" my father commanded as he pushed so strongly that David skidded slowly across the bed.

"I'm trying!"

"Try harder! You can't go there wearing one shoe and – there!"

David stood up and wiggled his foot around. "I just hope I can get it off afterwards."

"Where's Tristan?" my father asked, looking around the room.

"I'm here," Tristan said as he stepped into the room.

"Wow!" I gasped.

Tristan was dressed in a fancy dark suit and had an even fancier bow tie around his neck. His hair was all gelled and done up.

"It takes a little longer to get perfection . . . not that any of you guys would know."

"Pretty sharp, Tristan," my father said.

Tristan did a little twirl like he was a model on a runway, holding his jacket slightly open to reveal the shirt.

"I still think you look like you belong on the top of a wedding cake," Jamie commented.

"Jealousy . . . nothing but jealousy speaking."

"Okay, so everybody's ready . . . where's Kia?" my father asked.

I looked around the room. I'd forgotten all about her.

"I'm in here!" she called out from behind the closed bathroom door.

"We're all ready to go," I called back. "Are you dressed yet?"

"I'm not going anywhere!" she yelled back.

"Of course you are!" my father called out through the door. "Come on, Kia, we have to go! Are you dressed?"

"I'm dressed, and that's the problem!"

"What do you mean . . . how is that a problem?" my father asked.

"You wouldn't believe what she packed for me!" she said through the still closed door.

"It can't be that bad," my father suggested.

"Yes, it is!"

"Come on out and let us see," my father said.

"I'm not coming out!" she protested. "Nobody's going to see me dressed like this!"

"Kia, be reasonable. We have to go. Just come out and let's see . . . it can't be that bad."

There was no response from behind the door.

"Come on, Kia," my father pleaded. "We don't want to be late."

"Okay . . . I'll come out . . . but nobody better laugh."

"Nobody is going to laugh."

"They better not," she said.

I heard the lock click, and the door slowly started to open. Kia stepped out even slower. I gasped. She was wearing a short, pink, summer dress. It was covered in little blue flowers. On her feet were white platform sandals. She looked . . . she looked . . . completely un-Kialike.

"Okay, let's hear your stupid comments," she said.

Nobody said a word. I think we were all too stunned to say anything.

"I've never . . . um . . . seen you in a dress before," Jamie stammered.

"Neither have I," I agreed, and I was thinking of all the way back to when we were in kindergarten together. "I didn't even know you *owned* a dress."

Tristan chuckled. "I didn't even know you were a girl."

"Shut up or I'll — " Kia started to threaten and then fell forward off her platform shoes, landing in Mark's arms. They both struggled and strained to disengage themselves from each other and get her back on her feet.

"Everybody just stop!" my father yelled, and the room fell silent.

"I don't care what anybody thinks or says," he continued. "I think you look just . . . just — "

"Beautiful," Mark said, his voice just above a whisper.

Everybody turned and stared at Mark.

"Is that a crack?" Kia demanded.

Mark turned beet red and stared down at his feet.

"No, you *do* look beautiful!" my father agreed.

"Yeah, you look sort of like — "

"And I don't want to hear a word from you especially!" Kia said, cutting off Tristan.

"Me? Why me?"

"Because you're the only one here who's dressed even stupider than me," Kia snapped.

"I'm not dressed stupid!" he protested. "I'm sharp and stylish is what I am!"

"Enough, enough! You're all dressed wonderfully, and we're not going to talk anymore about it!" my father yelled. "All of you out into the hall . . . now!"

Kia opened her mouth to protest, but my father's angry gaze made her think better of saying anything. My father opened the door and pointed out into the hall.

David limped forward. Mark followed behind, still staring at his feet, avoiding any possibility of making eye contact with Kia. Tristan came next, head up, sort of strutting as he walked. Next, Kia stumbled, putting a hand against the dresser to steady herself. She mumbled something under her breath, but kept going.

Jamie looked at me. "Great, all we need is

for her to fall down and sprain an ankle or something," he whispered.

I shrugged in response. Jamie and I followed after them. My father shut the door behind us, as he was the last to leave the room.

Chapter Six

Coach Barkley stood in the hall, arms folded across his chest, surrounded by the other half of the team. All six guys stood there with their mouths open, staring at Kia. She had a scowl glued to her face. I knew she was just waiting for somebody to say something.

"Kia," Coach said. "You look really nice."

"Mark used the word beautiful," Tristan added.

Mark looked down even harder at the floor, and unbelievably his face turned an even brighter shade of red.

"I do believe that Mark is right," Coach said. "She looks downright beautiful. Don't you boys all agree?"

There were a few mumbled comments and nodding of heads. She *did* look really nice . . .

different than I'd ever seen her before.

"Actually, you all look handsome. You guys clean up pretty good . . . a lot better than I expected," Coach said.

"I just wish their mothers were all here to see how good they look," my father said. "We have to take some pictures just to prove it."

"Don't worry about pictures," Coach said. "There'll be lots and lots of pictures taken at the reception. Let's get down there."

We followed Coach to the elevator. Just as we arrived it pinged. Loud voices and laughter flowed out as the doors started to open to reveal a whole group of boys standing inside. They were dressed in matching shirts and ties.

"No room in here . . . take the next one!" a voice called out.

"No problem," my father called back.

The doors started to slide shut again. "Maybe there's room for the girl," somebody called out, followed by giggles as the door closed completely.

"Stupid jerk!" Kia snapped.

"We'll see them downstairs and — "

"And what?" Coach demanded, interrupting Tristan.

"And . . . and thank them for offering to let Kia on the elevator."

"That's all we're going to be doing," Coach said. "Lots of the teams here are going to be talking trash, both off and on the court. We're not getting into it. I'm counting on people to control their tempers, understand?"

"Sure, no problem," Tristan agreed.

"I'm more worried about other people," he said. "Kia?"

"Me?" she asked innocently. "You don't have to worry about me."

"Good."

The elevator pinged again and the door opened, revealing another completely filled compartment.

"Let's take the stairs," Coach said.

"But we're on the eleventh floor," L.B. said.

"But we're walking *down*, not climbing *up*," Coach said. "If that's too much work maybe you should sit on the bench for the first game."

"I think I'm okay," L.B. said.

"Besides, it'll give everybody a chance to get the blood flowing in their legs again," my father said. "After that long ride we could all use a little exercise."

We filed after the coach down to the other end of the hall to where the "stairs" sign glowed red. He pushed open the door and we all went into the stairwell. The sound of our feet echoed loudly as we all thundered down the stairs. I looked back over my shoulder, up to the landing. Kia was gingerly making her way down the stairs, one hand holding onto the railing.

She looked down at me. "Do you think it's easy getting around in these things?" she asked, holding one sandaled foot in the air.

"Just be careful," I said.

"Will you at least wait up?" Kia asked.

"Sure . . . no problem," I said as everybody continued down the stairs, leaving us farther and farther behind, the sounds of their voices and feet disappearing down the stairwell beneath us.

"I feel so stupid," Kia said. "I look so stupid."

"You don't look stupid," I said.

"Of course, I do . . . don't I?"

I shook my head. "Seriously, you look okay."

"Just okay?" she asked.

"Okay . . . better than okay," I said. What exactly was it she wanted me to say, that she was beautiful? She'd be waiting a long time to hear that.

"Well . . . even if I look okay, I still feel stupid, and I'm going to feel stupid in front of hundreds of people."

"It'll be fine," I offered reassuringly. "It's not like you'll be alone. We'll all be there with you."

"Will you do me a favor?" she asked.

"I guess . . . sure . . . if you want . . . what's the favor?"

"When we get down to the reception . . . "

"Yeah?"

"Could you stay right there with me?" she asked.

"At the reception?"

She nodded her head.

"Why do you want me to do that?" I questioned.

"I just want you to!" she snapped.

"Sure, if that's what you want."

"Maybe not the whole time. Just let me see how it goes."

I nodded in agreement. "Are you feeling nervous?"

"No, of course not . . . maybe just a little."

I tried to stifle a laugh, but it came out.

"What are you laughing at?" she demanded.

"Nothing," I said.

"That's it, I'm not going down there," she said, turning on her heel and starting back up the stairs.

"Kia!" I called out, and bounded after her. She moved so slowly in the sandals that I caught up with her before she'd gone no more than a few steps. I grabbed her by the arm.

"You have to come down," I pleaded.

"I'm not going down there to have all those people laugh at the way I'm dressed."

"I wasn't laughing at the way you're dressed, honestly!"

"Then what were you laughing at?" she asked again.

"Well . . . it just seemed sort of funny that I'm usually the one who feels nervous about things

50

and today it's you. That's all."

"You'd be nervous too if you were dressed stupid."

"You think I like wearing this get-up?" I asked, referring to my dress clothes and tie.

"I'd trade you in a second," she said, and then burst into laughter.

"Now, what are *you* laughing at?" I demanded.

"I was just thinking of you wearing this dress . . . or even better, Mark. I'd just go right up to him and tell him how *beautiful* he looked."

"I don't know," I said, "but I don't think Mark would look that good in a dress."

"Probably not, but why did he have to go and say that about me?"

I swallowed hard. "I don't think he was trying to make fun of you."

"Then why did he say it?" she asked.

I swallowed even harder. "Maybe that's what he thought."

"That I look beautiful?"

I nodded my head. I really, really didn't like where this was going.

"And what do you think?" Kia asked.

"I don't know . . . I hadn't really thought about it and — "

"Nick . . . Kia?" my father's voice came echoing up the stairwell.

"We're up here!" I yelled back.

"Hurry up!" he called out. "Everybody else is waiting by the door to the reception hall. I'll wait for you down here at the bottom!"

"We have to go, Kia," I said.

"Okay," she agreed.

We started down the stairs. I led and looked back over my shoulder. Kia kept one hand on the railing as she carefully, and slowly, moved down the stairs. It looked like walking was a real effort, and she was very deliberate as she placed a foot on each step.

"I don't know why my mother packed these things," Kia said.

"You didn't know she'd put those things in the bag?" I asked.

She shook her head. "She always packs my bag — correction. She always *used* to pack my bag."

"But you knew we had to have dressy clothes," I said, "so what did you think she was going to pack for you?"

"Dressy clothes doesn't mean a dress, you know. The first time I ever saw this dress is when I opened up my bag. She must have gone out special to get it. Why would she do something like that?"

I had a few ideas. Kia's mother was pretty cool about Kia being in basketball, but I'd once overheard her telling my mother that sometimes she wished that Kia did more "girl" things. I'd never told anybody, even Kia — *especially* Kia — about what I'd heard.

Besides, as far as I was concerned, "girl" things were anything a girl wanted to do. This wasn't like the olden days when boys played sports and the only thing girls played was dolls. Of course, the same was true for boys. If a boy wanted to take up dancing that was all right with me. Not that I'd ever admit it to anybody, but I would love to bust a move the way those guys in rock videos do.

"I feel like such a *girl* in this get-up," Kia said.

"Kia, I'd hoped you'd noticed before this, but you *are* a girl."

"I know I'm a girl, but I'm not a *girl*."

"Do you want to run that one by me again?" I asked.

"What don't you understand? I know I'm a girl, like female, but that doesn't mean I have to be a *girl*."

"Gee, thanks for explaining that so clearly," I snapped.

"Sometimes you're so dense," she said, and let out a big sigh. "It's simple. I'm female, but I'm not like those stupid girls – you know the ones in our class – who wear dresses, and read stupid fashion magazines and wear nail polish and act so . . . so . . . *girly*. Can't you just picture

53

Mandi or Amy in this dress?"

I actually could picture them wearing Kia's dress because those two almost always wore dresses to school.

"So do you understand now?" Kia questioned.

"I think I get the idea," I admitted.

"What took you two so long?" my father asked as we hit the bottom of the stairwell.

"You wanna try to walk in these things?" Kia questioned.

"I still think you look lovely. You should think about dressing like that more often," my father suggested.

Kia glared at him with a look that could have melted metal, but she kept her mouth shut. She took a couple of steps and tripped, my father grabbing onto her as she started to tumble toward the floor.

"Gotcha!" my father called out as he made the catch.

"Stupid shoes!" Kia muttered.

"You just have to get used to them. Your mother wears heels, doesn't she?" my father asked.

"All the time."

"Haven't you ever tried them on?" my father asked.

"I don't know."

"Come on, you must have," my father said. "I remember Nick used to wear his mother's shoes all the time."

"When I was little!" I protested. "Really little!"

"Maybe we should trade shoes," Kia joked.

"Forget that! It'll be like walking on stilts and . . . you have stilts, Kia."

She shrugged. "So?"

"Your stilts are really high and you hardly ever fall off them. What's so different about these?" I asked.

"They're a lot different. Besides, the reason I don't fall off the stilts is because I concentrate."

"Then maybe you have to concentrate when you wear these sandals," I suggested. "Don't think about anything but walking. It might work."

Kia shrugged again. That was her way of saying that maybe I was right without actually *saying* that maybe I was right.

My father held open the door and Kia exited the stairwell. I trailed behind. The door entered onto the main lobby. The place was packed. Everywhere I looked there were little clusters or large groups of boys — guys our age. Most seemed to be dressed pretty much like we were — shirts that looked too tight around the neck and badly tied ties. Some wore uncomfortable-looking dress shoes, but others were just wearing their basketball shoes.

As we moved around the groups, it quickly became apparent that Kia was being watched.

Kids and adults stopped talking or joking around and turned and watched as she passed by. I think Kia was so busy concentrating on walking without tripping that she didn't seem to notice. That was a good thing.

We caught up to the coach and the guys standing in front of a big set of double doors.

"Okay, everybody, let's do this as a team. We walk into the banquet hall in twos . . . I lead. Follow me to our table. Kia . . . Nick, you're the first two right behind me."

Chapter Seven

I opened my mouth in awe of the room we'd just entered. It was gigantic and filled with large circular tables. The ceiling stretched up into the heights — at the very center it became a dome that must have been three or four stories high. I didn't think I'd ever seen a room this fancy, except for maybe on television.

The tables were starting to fill up with people. Each table was set with dishes and glasses and lots and lots of knives and forks and had a big centerpiece made of flowers set around a miniature basketball. At the top of each centerpiece was a sign that identified who was supposed to sit at that table. It had the name of the club and where it was from. As we passed I looked at the signs.

Of course I didn't recognize the names of the clubs, but the cities were hard not to know: Detroit, Philadelphia, L.A., New York. I didn't actually know anybody who lived in any of those cities, but I did know that a whole lot of the very best players in the NBA were born and raised in those places. Which meant that at one point those NBA players were kids my age who had maybe played for rep teams like these kids did. It was sort of exciting to think that I might be playing against some kid who'd be in the NBA some day. Exciting, but scary.

As far as I knew our city had produced a couple of pretty good hockey players, but no big-league basketball superstars. About as close as we came was our coach — my dad said he would have been a star if he hadn't been injured and forced to retire.

"Here's our table," Coach Barkley said.

It was right up close to the front, right by a long, raised table with a platform that looked sort of like a stage, and a podium with a microphone.

"Everybody take a seat," my father said.

The table was gigantic and had room for fourteen. We all scrambled for seats. I almost pulled Kia's chair out for her. That would have been really stupid.

"At least I can't fall off the chair," she said as she sat down beside me.

"You did well," I said. "You didn't even stumble once."

"I just hope none of the games we play will be as hard as walking to this table."

"Look!" Tristan yelled, pointing at the name in the middle of the table. "They spelled Mississauga wrong!"

Right there on the table it read, The Magic – from Misisaga.

"That's insulting," Kia said.

"They don't even know where we're from," Jamie agreed.

"Maybe they know, but can't spell it," L.B. suggested. "I was living there for almost three months before *I* could spell it."

"Either way," Coach said, "I'm going to fix it."

He reached into his pocket and pulled out a pen. He removed the sign from the centerpiece and flipped it over to hide the writing and reveal a blank surface. He started to write — big, dark, capital letters.

"This is better," he said as he held it up and showed it to us.

THE MISSISSAUGA MAGIC, it read.

Everybody gave a little round of applause as he took the sign and put it back in place with the flowers.

"I betcha nobody got *their* name wrong," Tristan

said as he pointed to a table directly behind me.

Without turning around, I knew which table he meant. It was just behind us and had two signs — one identified them as being the "Wild Cats from New York City." The other sign — bigger than the first — said "Defending Champions."

"New York is a lot easier to spell," I said.

"And a lot better known," Kia stated.

"Not to mention the defending champions," Tristan added.

"Not just the defending champions," Coach said. "The *four*-time defending champions."

"The four-time champions?" I questioned. "But this tournament is just for our age group . . . right?"

"That's right," Coach confirmed.

"So it can't be the same kids," I reasoned.

"That's right. Every year it's different kids from the same club, but with the same coach."

"He must be a pretty good coach," L.B. said.

Coach nodded his head. "Must be ... although it doesn't hurt that he draws from a developmental program and house league that has over four hundred teams."

"That is pretty big," my father admitted. "How many teams are there in the Magic organization?"

"I'm not sure exactly, but if you look at both girls' and boys' teams from beginners to the top level, there probably are around eighty teams," Coach said.

"So that means that the New York coach has about five times as many kids to choose from," my father reasoned.

"Five times?" Coach questioned. "You don't understand."

"What do you mean?" my father asked. "We have eighty and they have four hundred, so that's five times as big as — "

"I'm not talking about four hundred teams in the whole Wild Cat organization," Coach said. "I'm talking about four hundred teams of kids the *same age* as our boys."

"You're joking, right?" my father asked.

"No joke. They have leagues across the whole city, and it's the biggest city in North America. Mississauga may have six hundred thousand people, but compared to New York it's just a village."

"But a nice village," Tristan added.

"I like it," Kia agreed.

"Best place in the world to live, even if it is hard to spell," Jamie said.

"I don't think those guys would agree," I added.

Coming toward where we sat was a large group of large guys. Each wore an identical outfit: red, white and blue warm-ups with N.Y. emblazoned in big letters across the front. They had on sparkling white basketball shoes that looked like they were brand new. And to top everything off they all were wearing shades — dark, mirrored shades.

It certainly didn't seem that bright in here to me.

"They're our age?" David asked.

"If they're here, they're your age," Coach said.

They did seem big – awfully big. A couple of our guys, like Jordan and Al, and maybe Sean, could match up to them, but they were *huge*.

"Are they putting something in the drinking water in New York?" L.B. asked.

"You have enough kids to choose from you can get some pretty big players," Coach said. "But just because they're big doesn't mean they can play."

"But it doesn't mean they can't play, either," I replied.

"How come they got to wear warm-ups and we have to dress like this?" Jamie asked.

"We could have worn warm-ups too," Coach Barkley said.

"Then why didn't we?" Kia asked.

"Because I think warm-ups are for warming up, not for a reception. It just doesn't look professional."

"But it does look cool," L.B. said.

"Especially the sunglasses," Tristan added. "How about if we get some like that?"

"They'd be perfect," Coach said.

"They would?" L.B. questioned.

"Sure . . . if we were the Mississauga Magic

beach volleyball team."

We all watched as they filed past our table – sort of walking, sort of strutting, sort of gliding. They didn't say a word as they passed, but the way they passed said it all – it was like saying, "We're from New York and you're not."

David leaned over and whispered, "They wouldn't be acting so cool if they were dressed like us."

"Or like me," Kia added.

I broke out laughing and the last two New York players turned and looked at me — at least, I think they were looking at me — as they passed by. I stifled the laugh.

Coach Barkley suddenly stood up. "Hello, Coach," he said as he reached out his hand toward a little man at the end of the line – a man dressed in the identical warm-up suit as the players. "I'm Len Barkley, the coach of the Magic."

The man extended his hand. "Jeff Barton . . . coach of the Wild Cats," he said. "Your name sounds familiar . . . have you had a team here before?"

"This is my first year coaching, but I was here as a *player* over thirty years ago."

"Isn't that wonderful!" he beamed. "To be a player and then be a coach! Wonderful! And where is your team from?"

"Mississauga."

"Mmmm . . . I hate to admit my ignorance,

but I don't know where that is," he said.

"It's by Toronto," Coach said.

"It's a big city, almost six hundred thousand people," my father added. "Not New York big, but a nice-sized city."

"I'm sure it is," he said, although there was a tone in his voice like maybe he didn't really believe that. "So has your team been to many tournaments this year?"

"This is our first," Coach said.

"Your first?" he asked in disbelief. "They let you in here without playing in any other tournaments before this one?"

"I guess they liked our record from last year. Has your team been in many tournaments?"

"This will be our seventh."

"Seventh?" my father gasped, voicing my disbelief. "Our team hasn't even been together seven weeks."

"And how have you done?" Coach asked.

"Well, we could have played better, but we've done all right . . . if you consider winning every game and every tournament all right," he said with a smirk.

"Must be quite the team," Coach said.

"They're not bad. Maybe not as good as my last year's team, but we'll see how they are at the end of the season. Do you have other tournaments scheduled for your team?" he asked.

"A couple. We'll see how we do here," Coach said.

"I'm sure you'll do fine . . . just remember this is a pretty hard place to start . . . for both the players and a *beginning* coach."

For a split second I saw Coach Barkley's eyes blaze brightly, and then the look of anger was gone. "It certainly is a difficult beginning, but I hope we'll do all right."

"That's the attitude! And remember, if you have any questions or I can offer any assistance, you just find me and I'll help you out. Okay?"

"Thank you so much," Coach said. "That's so kind of you to — "

"Excuse me," a woman said. She was young and pretty and dressed in a blazer.

The two men turned to face her.

"I was wondering if it would be possible for me to get a short interview?" she asked.

Behind her were two men. One was holding a big camera on his shoulder and the other held two microphones.

"Sure," the New York coach said. "I've always got time for the press." He turned to Coach Barkley. "If you'll excuse me, we can talk later."

"No," the woman said. "You don't understand. I don't want to interview *you*, I want to interview *Coach Barkley*."

Chapter Eight

"Him? You want to interview him?" Coach Barton asked in amazement.

"Yes," she said.

"But . . . but I'm the coach of the defending champion team . . . the New York City Wild Cats."

"That's wonderful, really, and I know I'll get around to interviewing you at some point," she said.

"But you want to interview him first?" he asked, sounding completely mystified.

She nodded.

"I played a little ball around here," Coach said to the man, trying to explain.

"A little ball!" the reporter exclaimed. "You call leading your college team to three straight titles a *little* ball?"

"My team has won this tournament *four* straight times," the New York coach said.

"That is certainly impressive," the reporter agreed. "And that's why we'll interview you too . . . just not right now. So if you could please just move aside and let me interview Coach Barkley."

She placed a hand on his shoulder and sort of pushed him away a few steps. He reluctantly shuffled to the side. I looked at the expression on his face. It was a combination of disbelief and anger. Not only didn't he see this coming, but he was angry it had arrived.

All of a sudden I was hit by the glare of a bright light, and I brought a hand up to shield my eyes. The big light of the camera had been turned on and it was aimed at Coach. The reporter held the microphone in one hand while she ran the fingers of her other hand through her hair. Her hair was all poofed up and she wore lots and lots of make-up. She was the sort of girl who was a *girl*. I could see her wearing a bigger version of Kia's dress.

"Do I look all right?" she asked the cameraman.

"You look fine," he said. "Let's roll on this interview."

"Okay, I'm ready."

"Rolling in five . . . four . . . three . . . two . . . one," and then he pointed at her.

"This is Elyse Parris reporting from the thirty-seventh annual Mumford Basketball Tournament, which brings together the best young basketball players of today. And with me is a former participant in this tournament who went on to become a college star, play in the NBA and is now back as a coach to lead his team. With me is Len Barkley. Welcome."

"Thank you, Elyse."

"Len, how does it feel to be back here?"

"It feels pretty good."

"And just how many years ago was it that you were a player in this tournament?"

"More years than I care to remember or admit."

"Now we all know what happened in some of those years," the reporter said. "I don't imagine there's anybody around the country who followed college basketball who will ever forget you leading your team to those league championships."

"Those were good years," Coach said.

"And I'm sure that since your college ball was just down the road from here, you have plenty of local people who remember you fondly."

"And I have fond memories of them," he said, sounding more like a politician than a basketball coach.

"One of the strongest memories many people will have of your college days was, of course, the injury that ended it all."

"I remember that one pretty good myself."

"Do you have any thoughts about what might have been if that injury hadn't ended your career?" she asked.

"I used to think about what could have been all the time."

"Used to?"

Coach smiled. "It's been a long time. Besides, this tournament isn't about the past, but the future. I'm here with my team."

"And a fine-looking bunch they are," she said. Slowly the camera moved off the coach and the reporter and began to pan around the table.

"So tell me about your team."

"We're here representing the city of Mississauga."

"That's where you're originally from, is it not?" she asked.

"I was born in that area and recently moved back to Mississauga with my family."

"And is this team the champion in that city?" she asked.

"They represent the whole city . . . the best players of their age that Mississauga has to offer."

"They look like a fine group of boys," she said.

"Boys and *girl*," he corrected her.

"Girl?" she asked.

"Yes . . . this young lady at our table is a member of our team."

"Isn't that wonderful!" the reporter gushed. "I'd just assumed she was your daughter!"

The reporter moved over toward Kia – and me – and the camera followed right after.

"She's been a member of the Magic rep team for three years and plays either point or small forward," Coach explained.

"So tell us, Kia, how does it feel to be one of the only girls in this tournament?" the reporter asked.

"Um . . . I don't know," she muttered.

That didn't seem like Kia, to be at a loss for words, although I wasn't sure if I could say anything either. Something about having the bright lights of the camera pointed at you could dry up your words pretty quick.

"She's actually the *only* girl in this tournament and only the *second* girl in the history of this tournament," Coach explained.

"That makes it even more extraordinary!" the reporter gushed. "So, Kia, how long have you been playing basketball?"

"Um . . . as long as I can remember . . . even longer," she stammered.

"And what made you decide to play on a boys'

team?" she asked.

Kia shrugged. "I've always played on this team."

"Surely there must be girls' teams where you could play," the reporter said.

"Sure," Kia said.

"And those teams must compete in tournaments as well," the reporter continued.

"I guess so, but then I wouldn't be with my friends . . . I've always played with Nick."

"Nick?" the reporter asked.

"Nick is my best friend," Kia explained. "We've always been friends and played together and been on the same team."

"And which one of these boys is Nick?" the reporter asked.

"This is Nick," she said, tapping me on the arm.

I gave a weak little smile and waved, although the camera was still aimed directly at Kia.

"Has it been difficult playing with boys?" the reporter asked.

"Difficult?" Kia questioned. "I'm a better player than most of the boys!"

The reporter laughed out loud. "That's great to hear, but I didn't mean how you play, but are you ever given a hard time for playing with the boys?"

Kia shook her head. "Only a jerk would hassle me, and who cares what jerks think?"

Again the reporter laughed out loud. She then turned from Kia to face the camera directly.

"I was going to ask if you ever get accused of being to much of a tomboy, but no one could ever say that about the way that you're dressed," the reporter said.

I could see Kia's expression harden.

"Do you always dress so femininely?"

"You mean in a dress?" Kia asked.

"A very *lovely* dress," the reporter added.

"No . . . do you?" Kia questioned.

The reporter looked visibly thrown by Kia being the one to ask the question. She quickly recovered.

"We are certainly covering an interesting human interest story! Kia is one of only two females ever to compete in this tournament, and I'm sure we'll be following her – and her team – as the tournament continues. This is Elyse Parris for channel two news!"

"And cut!" called out the cameraman. He turned off the big light and lowered the camera.

"How did that go?" the reporter asked anxiously.

"It went fine . . . good," the cameraman replied.

"Excellent." She turned to face Coach. "I think there are outstanding possibilities for this story. What would you think about us following your team throughout the tournament?"

"You're certainly free to follow any team, including ours," he replied.

Wow, that would be amazing to have a TV reporter following us around! I could see by the expressions on everybody's faces that they thought the same thing. Tristan straightened his tie, like he was thinking the camera was coming right back on and he wanted to look his best. He did look pretty snazzy.

"How about right after the reception we set up another time to do more interviews and — "

"There won't be any more interviews tonight," Coach said.

"Why not?" she questioned.

"Because we're here to play basketball and not give interviews."

"But it won't take much time and — "

"It isn't a question of the time as much as the distraction the interview will cause, and we don't need any more distractions than this tournament already offers."

"I'll be brief, and besides, I'm going to mainly focus on Kia and — "

"Sorry," Coach said. "You've already interviewed her, and I really want this to be about the team, not any individual."

"But you have to admit that Kia certainly is a *unique* member of your team."

"There are many unique members of this team," Coach said.

"But you said yourself that she is one of only a few girls who have — "

"One of only *two* girls," Coach corrected her.

"Yes, two girls," the reporter said. "One of only two girls who have ever competed in this, the most prestigious tournament for youngsters in the entire country."

"And I'm sure it would make wonderful news," Coach agreed, "but we're not here to make news. We're here to play ball."

"Certainly, but wouldn't your players, wouldn't Kia, enjoy being the subject of our interviews?"

"I just want to play basketball," Kia said.

Coach gave a big smile. "You heard what she said."

"How about tomorrow?" she persisted. "Could we have a few minutes tomorrow?"

"We're busy tomorrow," Coach said. "We're playing in a basketball tournament."

"What about at the end of the tournament?" she asked.

"After all the games are over?" Coach asked. The reporter nodded.

"I'm not saying no . . . but I'm not saying yes. Let's just see how it goes."

"It wouldn't be a distraction then and — "

"Could everybody please take their seats, we're

about to begin!" called out a loud, amplified voice.

I spun around in my seat. There was a man standing just in front of us by the podium. The long table at the front was now filled. Scanning the whole room, I noticed that almost all the tables were now packed, and those seats that were empty quickly started to fill.

"It sounds like we're going to have to stop now," Coach said.

"Maybe we can talk afterwards," the reporter pressed.

"After the reception, no," Coach said. "After the tournament . . . maybe."

Chapter Nine

"Good evening and welcome to the thirty-seventh annual Mumford International Invitational Basketball Tournament," the man at the microphone called out.

There were cheers and hoots in reply.

"My name is Mike Riley and I'll be the master of ceremonies for tonight as well as the chief official for the tournament. In addition, I am the mayor of Mumford, and as such I want to formally welcome you to our fine city!"

A round of applause rose from the crowd and we joined in, even though I wasn't exactly sure why.

"We take great pride in our tournament and particular pride in our Mumford team – who you'll meet during the course of the reception. Now, I want you all to look around," he continued. "Gathered around you in this room are the very best basketball players of your age from across North America."

A shudder went up my spine. Here we were with the very best . . . did we even deserve to be here?

"And," the speaker continued, "showing the global impact of basketball, this year we have teams from both Europe and Asia!"

"Asia?" Kia asked. "I knew about Europe but not Asia."

Coach leaned forward. "There's a team from Japan and one from Korea."

That was amazing. I looked around the room trying to see if I could find one.

"Could I ask the team from France, the team from England, the team from Korea and the Japanese team to please stand up?"

To the sound of scraping chairs, the players at two tables at the back, one close to the door and a table just over from us rose to their feet.

"Let's give them all a big round of applause for coming so far!"

We all politely clapped and the players sort of bowed and then sat back down.

Kia leaned toward me. "Was that the team

from Japan over there?" she asked, pointing to the nearest table that had risen.

I shrugged. "Japanese or Korean, I guess . . . at least, they sort of looked Japanese or Korean."

She nodded. "I thought they'd be shorter."

"Everybody's big here. Everybody."

"And," the announcer continued, "since we have so many teams present, I think it's best to get things rolling. The first step is the introduction of the teams."

That was important. I was anxious to know which teams we'd be competing against in the first round. Then again, what did it matter? It wasn't like there were going to be any soft spots.

"We'll begin with the Condors, from Cleveland, Ohio! Let's give them a nice round of applause to welcome them up here!"

One of the teams from a table near the back of the room all rose to their feet and started to walk toward the front of the banquet hall as people clapped.

"What are they doing?" I asked.

"Coming up to the podium to be introduced," Coach replied.

"You're joking . . . right?" I asked.

He shook his head. "The coach will introduce the players and say a few words."

"Are we going to do that?"

"*Every* team does."

"But there are forty teams here; that could take hours!" Kia said.

"If things go well, it'll only take about two and half hours," Coach said.

The team from Cleveland all gathered together on the little stage behind the microphone. They looked as uncomfortable as I thought I would. What could be worse than being dressed like a goof in front of hundreds of strangers? Then again, it was better to be dressed this way in front of strangers than people you knew – people that could make fun of you later.

Their coach shook hands with Mr. Riley and then stepped up to the microphone.

"Greetings from the great state of Ohio," he began. "I'm proud to introduce my team, most of whom were on my team last year when we won the state championship for our age!"

Great . . . just great. I looked over at Kia to say something, but she was staring up at the stage. She didn't look as impressed as I felt.

The coach went on to introduce his players, one by one. They looked like players . . . nothing really special, but they looked like ball players. But then again, what had I been expecting?

"Let's give them all another round of applause," Mayor Riley said. We clapped as the team left the stage and started back to their table.

"I'd now like to introduce the next team. Let's

give a big round of applause for the Suns from Seattle!"

I started clapping my hands together, but not as enthusiastically as for the first team. If I had to do this for forty teams, my hands would be worn out before the tournament even began.

"Only thirty-nine to go," Kia said.

"Including us," I added.

"Do we know when we're going to be called?" L.B. asked his father.

"They don't tell the teams. About the only thing I know is that we won't be last."

"There's a *chance* we could be last," L.B. said.

Coach shook his head. "The New York team will be last because they're technically the defending champions."

The second team had reached the podium and their coach began to speak.

Kia leaned close. "Wake me when it's our turn," she said.

"I was going to say the same thing," I whispered back.

"How many teams are left to introduce?" Tristan asked as we clapped our hands for yet another team leaving the podium.

"Three left," my father said.

"Are you sure?" Tristan asked.

"I'm sure . . . believe me . . . I've been counting."

"Then we could be next," Kia said.

"We could have been next every time," I said. "Either way, we're not going to be much longer."

I looked at my watch. It was coming up to nine-thirty. We'd been sitting here for almost two and a half hours.

I'd tried my best to pay attention as team after team walked forward, was introduced and left, but I couldn't help but drift off. I even started to think about the possibility of sinking further and further down in my seat until I could maybe slide under the table. From there I could crawl from table to table and maybe make a break for the door. This was like sitting in school listening to a really, really bad teacher just go on and on about something stupid. The only thing that had kept me awake at all was the meal they brought us halfway through the introductions. The food had been good. I hoped we still wouldn't be sitting here when breakfast time rolled around.

"And next up is our team from Osaka, Japan. Let's give them a big welcome to our country!" the mayor announced.

We did our best to cheer them on. I'd never clapped so much in my life and been entertained so little. The team filed up to the front. Other groups had come in clumps or slunk or strutted as they came up to the podium. This group seemed to be almost marching. And since they had on identical warm-up suits, headbands and sneakers – very expensive sneakers – they looked like they were a little army all decked out in their uniforms.

Their coach came to the podium. He bowed his head slightly and then began.

"Excuse English . . . still learning. We are honored to be here. My team is still much to learn about English and basketball and hope you will teach us much. Thank you," he said, and bowed again.

There was the usual ripple of polite applause and he began to introduce the members of his team. Each in turn took a step forward, bowed his head when called out and then returned to his place in the line.

"They certainly are polite," Kia said.

"And disciplined and well coached," Coach said.

"How can you tell that?" I questioned.

"Just look at them," he said. "The way they walk, the way they present themselves."

I watched as they began to leave the stage. It was all done with the same precision that had brought them up to the podium. I guess I could understand what he was saying.

"We are now down to our last two teams," the master of ceremonies announced, and a cheer rose from the crowd — the first real cheering that had happened for the past hour.

"Could the Magic of Mississauga, led by former college star and NBA player Len Barkley, please come on up!" he called out.

We all pushed out our chairs and got up. Maybe it was my imagination, but there seemed to be more cheering than there had been for a long time. I wondered if everybody was clapping because they were so grateful that we were finally close to the end, then remembered about Coach playing his college ball around here.

I took a step forward and felt myself stumble slightly. We'd been sitting so long one of my legs was partially asleep. I couldn't help but think that we certainly weren't walking up with the precision of the team from Japan.

I looked up to the table on the podium. All the men seated up at the front were cheering wildly, and three of them were on their feet applauding. This certainly wasn't the way they'd greeted the other teams. As we climbed up the steps to reach the stage, the men who were standing rushed over and shook Coach's hand. The mayor pumped his hand like he was hoping to get his vote in the next election. Coach went over to the podium.

"Thank you all for your warm greetings," Coach said. "I'm thrilled to be here today with my team.

As the mayor mentioned, I played some college ball and even had the privilege of playing in the NBA for a short while. But the memories that are most dear to me are those from when I was first starting out . . . playing ball with my teammates and coming to tournaments just like this. Now I'd like to introduce the members of my team."

I stood there feeling anxious and awkward as he called out each name, starting from the far end. I was going to be second last and Kia, who was standing beside me, was at the end. Finally he called out my name and I took a step forward – the way I'd seen close to four hundred other kids do before me.

"And finally I'd like to introduce my last player," Coach said. "Kia . . . she plays guard and small forward."

Kia stepped forward and it was like the entire room gasped. Standing up there in her flowery dress, there wasn't much doubt that she was a girl – the only girl in the whole tournament.

"Thank you all," Coach said.

We stepped off the stage and started back to our seats while people applauded for the second to last time. It was loud and I knew that it was aimed more at Coach than it was at us.

"And thank you, Coach Barkley, for introducing your team . . . certainly your team is different in at least one way from the other teams," Mayor

85

Riley said. "I'd now like to introduce the fortieth and final team. From New York City, the four-time defending champions, the Wild Cats, led by their coach Jeff Barton!"

The team got up and started to the front. They walked up to the stage with that same sort of strut that had brought them into the banquet hall in the first place. It was also obvious that the applause for them wasn't nearly as loud as the cheering had been for us. I guess one former NBA player and college hero was worth more than the four-time defending champions.

The Wild Cat coach walked up to the podium as his team — all still wearing their sunglasses — took their places on the podium.

He began to speak. "It's not every day that I get to speak after a genuine *celebrity*."

There was something about the way he said celebrity that caused the hair on the back of my neck to stand up on end. I looked over at Coach. He had a smile frozen on his face.

"I'm very glad to be back here again," the Wild Cat coach continued. "This is my seventh time that I've brought a team to this tournament. As you all know, the last four times we left with the championship. Twice before that my team left with a second- and a third- place finish," the coach said. "Now, I may not have ever been a star in college or played in the NBA," he said, and then paused. "But *I* know how to coach."

That was obviously a shot aimed at Coach, and everybody in the whole place must have known that. It was like saying that just because he could play the game it didn't mean that he could coach the game.

I looked over at Coach. His face was still locked up with that same expression, although it seemed that the smile was just a little bit too tight. I'd seen the Coach angry — I'd seen him really, really angry — and this guy was a fool for trying to deliberately get him mad. Even if he didn't really know Coach, he must have known his reputation from when he was a player.

It was way before my time, but I was told that as a player our coach never took any prisoners. People, including my father, said he was probably the most intense player they'd ever seen in the game. My father said that if it weren't for that injury in his last year of college, he would have not only been playing in the NBA for years, but would have been a star.

"And my team knows how to play and how to win," Coach Barton continued, "and that's what we're here to do. Win!"

Chapter Ten

I looked up at the big board. The forty teams had been divided into eight pools — five teams to a pool. I anxiously scanned the groupings. I'd been thinking so much about which teams were going to be where that it had invaded my dreams, and when I woke up in the morning it was the first thing that popped into my head. I didn't really know any of the other teams — it wasn't like I'd ever seen anybody else play — but I knew one team I didn't want to be with: the Wild Cats from New York. I scanned the lists, looking for our team and their team. There they were — the Wild Cats — in pool B. And we weren't one of the other four teams in their division.

At least we didn't have to face them in the

first round. Maybe we wouldn't have to face them at all. Maybe they wouldn't get through the first round. Just because they were the four-time defending champions, and they'd already won every tournament they'd been in this year, and they were from New York, and they had really, really, cool sunglasses, didn't mean that they were any good . . . Who was I kidding?

It was a lot more likely that we wouldn't be facing them because we weren't going any further than the first round. I tried to put that thought out of my head. We were a good team. We were. I just knew, though, that if we kept winning we'd eventually meet them. One way or another, the team that wanted to be the champions of this tournament would have to go straight through the Wild Cats.

"There we are!" Kia called out. "Pool E."

I moved over beside her and joined other members of our team looking up at the board.

"Do you recognize any of the teams?" I asked.

"How would I know any of them?" she asked.

"I meant from the reception. Any teams that you can remember seeing last night?"

"Um . . . no . . . I don't think so . . . wait," she said, tapping the board. "Is that the team from France?"

"Unless there's another Paris somewhere else

in the world it has to be them," Tristan said.

"We should be able to beat a team from France," L.B. said.

"Do they even play basketball in France?" David asked.

"They have to or they wouldn't be here," Kia said.

"I know that, but I mean I thought they only played soccer or stuff like that," he said.

"You mean the way that people in Canada only play hockey?" I suggested.

"I guess you're right," David admitted.

"And I figure we'll find out if they can play basketball pretty soon," L.B. said. "They're our opponents in the first game."

"How long before we play?" I asked.

"About two hours. Everybody's first game is at noon," Kia said. "Every team plays at the same time to start the tournament. That means there are twenty games in twenty gyms."

"That must be every gym in town," Jamie said.

"Every one of them," Coach Barkley said as he and my father came up behind us. "Every school, the community college and the recreation center.

"And they'll be in use all day. By nine o'clock tonight the first round will be over and every team will have played four games."

"That's a lot of ball in one day," L.B. said.

"Four games is a lot," Coach agreed. "But we have a deep bench. Everybody will see a lot of action."

"How many teams get through from each pool?" Jamie asked.

"One," Coach said, holding up a single finger. "So we have to win our pool, and the only way that's guaranteed is if we win all four games."

"And if we get through this round what happens next?" David asked.

"Correction," Kia said. "*When* we get through this round."

"The second round is straight elimination. Only eight teams make it through. You lose, you go home. You win, you go on."

"How many games?" I asked.

"Three. The third one is for the championship," Coach said.

"So," Tristan said, "all we have to do is win four games today and three tomorrow and we're the champions."

"That's all," Coach said. "Seven wins and you're the winners of the tournament."

"That doesn't seem too hard," Tristan said. "We can do that."

"I hope we can, but right now let's just focus on the first game."

"Where do we play our first game?" Kia asked.

"The local community college. We're lucky,

we play all four of our games at the same place. It has three gyms," Coach explained.

"And that's on the other side of town, so maybe we better get ready and get going," my father suggested.

"Couldn't have said it better myself," Coach said. "Let's get going."

We had started to walk toward the elevators when we practically bumped into the New York team and coach.

"So," Coach Barton said, "we're in different pools for the first round."

"I guess we are," Coach replied.

"Lucky for them," one of the New York players said under his breath, but loud enough for us to hear.

"And the local team isn't in your division either," Coach Barton said. "That's a good sign."

"Are they that good?" my father asked.

Both Coach Barton and Coach chuckled. "This tournament has a reputation for trying to get their local team as far as they can every year."

"How does that work?" my father questioned.

"They usually put them in a weaker division," Coach said.

"And the officiating can be a little one-sided," Coach Barton said. "But either way, it's not going to affect *us*."

The way he said that made it seem like while his

team needn't worry, maybe we should be concerned.

"So, maybe, we'll be seeing your team later on in the tournament," Coach said. "Hopefully, the finals."

Coach Barton laughed. "Even *I* didn't get that far my first time, but that's the attitude! Now we all better get going."

We started off again for the elevators.

"I don't like that guy," I quietly said to Kia.

"I don't like any of those guys," she replied. "They just think they're really something. And you know what bothers me even more?"

"What?"

"I'm afraid they might be as good as they think they are."

I looked around the gym. It was one of three large gyms at the college. Two were simply created by a big curtain that was drawn across the middle to form the two separate gyms. The third gym, the one where we were scheduled to play, was separate. It was the biggest gym in all of Mumford, and we were told that this was where the semifinals and finals were held. All along one side was a large set of bleachers. There must have been room for thousands and thousands of fans. Thank goodness almost all the seats were empty. There couldn't have been any more than

three or four hundred people in the stands . . .
three or four hundred . . . that was pretty amazing all by itself for a game being played this
early in the morning.

"Nick, are you coming or not?" my father asked.
He was sitting at the end of the bench, filling
out the game sheet.

I looked at the court. Coach was just getting
ready to start the warm-ups. Everybody else was
already on the court, stretching and shooting,
waiting for Coach to begin. Quickly I pulled off
my warm-up jersey, grabbed my ball and headed
out.

As I dribbled out, I scuffed my feet against
the floor. They squeaked loudly. I loved that sound.
But even better than the sound was what the
sound meant – the floor was good and I wouldn't
be sliding around. Basketball was hard enough
without the floor being slippery. Sometimes when
we played it was more like figure skating than
basketball. But not here — this was a great gym.

I put up a shot and it dropped straight away.
Instinctively I looked up into the stands for my
mother and father. Then, of course, I realized
my dad had his head down, busily filling out
the game sheet, and my mother was hundreds
of miles away. She wasn't up there watching.
Actually, nobody that I knew was here cheering
us on.

Then I looked over and realized that we did know one person. Standing off to the side, just over from our bench, was that reporter. She was bathed in the bright light of the camera, which spilled past her and onto the side of the court where we were warming up.

"Okay, everybody, let's go!" Coach bellowed. "Two lines for lay-ups!"

I rolled my ball toward the bench and joined the line that was rebounding. Kia settled in behind me.

"You see your friend?" I asked.

"Hard to miss. She tried to get me to leave the warm-ups for an interview. Coach practically bit her head off."

"And?" I asked.

"She was smart enough to leave. She bothers me."

"Why, what did she do?" I asked.

"It's this whole story. She doesn't want to interview me because I'm a good basketball player, but because I'm a girl."

"Actually, Kia, you're both."

"I know that, but she doesn't," she snapped. "She doesn't even care if I'm any good and — Nick, you're next."

In the other line Jordan started dribbling in, and it was my turn to grab the rebound. He put the ball in, I took the rebound and fed it out to the next player coming in. I then joined the end of the line taking the shots.

Coach broke us up into another drill and then another and another. A couple of times people screwed up, and he said something sharper and louder than I expected. I was wondering if we'd see the new and improved coach or the guy who couldn't control his temper – the guy that none of us had wanted to play for. Just what I needed . . . something else to think about.

"Bring it in!" Coach bellowed, and we went over to the bench.

Quickly we grabbed our water bottles and then gathered around him.

"Here we are," he began. "Biggest tournament any of you have ever been in. How many of you have butterflies in the pit of your stomach?"

Nobody said a word. Reluctantly I raised my hand a little.

Coach looked confused. "You mean to tell me that Nick and I are the only two people who are nervous?"

That felt good. Slowly everybody else nodded their heads or raised a hand or said they felt a bit nervous.

"But that doesn't mean we're not going to take them," Tristan said. "We're a lot better."

"And what makes you think that?" Coach asked.

"I've been watching them during the warm-ups."

"That would explain why you weren't paying much attention to our warm-ups."

Tristan looked down at his sneakers.

"And what did you see?"

"Their center is tall, but he has no jump," Tristan said. "Jordan's going to eat him alive."

"I'd rather have a burger," Jordan joked.

"Anybody else see anything?" Coach asked.

"They can shoot from the outside," Jamie said. "Particularly from the three-point line."

Coach nodded.

"But it looked like they were taking a long time to get their shots off," L.B. added. "I think they can shoot good *if* we give them enough time."

"So?" Coach asked.

"So we can't give them time for a good look," L.B. said.

Coach nodded his head. "Anything else?"

Nobody answered.

"Nick, you're always watching the other team during the warm-ups. What did you notice?" Coach asked.

I was startled out of my thoughts. Actually, I'd been so distracted during the warm-ups that I'd hardly noticed there was a team at the other end of the gym. I could have told him all about the stands and the number of people and the reporter.

"Well?"

"I didn't see anything . . . except what's been mentioned. What did you see?" I asked.

It's always a good strategy to ask a question when you don't have an answer for the question you've been asked.

Coach smiled and chuckled. "Nice that somebody wants to know what I saw." He paused. "They have twelve players on their squad. Five look to be first class. From there the talent drops off sharply."

"So we have to get to their bench," Kia said.

Coach nodded. "We want to wear their starters out by making them work for every basket. I don't want any uncontested outside shooting because those points come too easily. I noticed that almost all their warm-up drills were focused on outside shooting. I don't think this team likes to go inside. I watched both their big men repeatedly fumble the ball. That means they're not going to be reliable targets for inside passes. They're going to win or lose from the outside."

"They're going to *lose* from the outside," Tristan said.

"That certainly is the *idea*. Now I'm going to tell you the *plan*," Coach said. "We're going to spend the whole game in a full court press."

"The whole game!" Kia exclaimed.

"Yes, the whole game. And if they manage to beat the press we're going to go with four men playing man to man with our big man staying under the hoop. We're going to force them to put the ball on the floor and drive or put the ball inside. We're going to make them play our game. Understood?"

Everybody nodded or voiced agreement.

"I'm starting four small, and one big. I expect everybody is going to be running flat out the whole time, pushing, pressing, fast breaking. Expect no shift will last more than two minutes because we're going to be making rapid and frequent changes."

That all made sense. Run them silly.

"Okay, starters are Jordan, Jamie, Tristan, Al and Nick. I need two minutes of flat-out fury that'll have that team thinking that the jet they traveled over on was slow compared to our team."

The ref blew his whistle, signaling that it was just about time to begin.

"Now remember," Coach said. "Nobody is going to live or die because of this game. We're here to play some basketball and have some fun . . . but remember . . . winning is *really* fun. Now break!"

Chapter Eleven

"Time out!" Coach yelled.

The five players on the floor, as well as the rest of us on the bench, gathered around him.

"There's under ten minutes left in this game and there's no way they're coming back," Coach said.

We were up by an even twenty points, so what he was saying couldn't have been truer. We'd pressed and pressed and pressed harder, and they had gotten nothing but more frustrated.

"Should we drop back to zone?" L.B. asked.

"Why should we stop doing what worked?" Coach asked.

L.B. shrugged. "We've already won, so do we have to kill them?"

"Yes, we do," his father said. "The second tie breaker in this round is most points scored."

"What's the first?" L.B. asked.

"Head-to-head play. We beat this team and even if we end up with the same record, we'd go through and they wouldn't. But just in case, we want more points . . . we *need* more points."

"No problem, Coach," Tristan said. "How many you want?"

"Thirty."

"You mean you want us to win by thirty or you want us to go up by *another* thirty?" Tristan asked.

"Win by thirty. I want to beat them, but I don't want to completely kill them . . . not completely."

Winning by thirty certainly seemed like a complete kill to me.

"Besides, we're not just trying to win this game. We're sending a message to every other team in the tournament that we're for real . . . that we're a team they should be afraid to play. Okay, same five players back on," Coach said.

Those players went back onto the floor while the rest of us – except Coach – settled onto the bench. He hadn't sat down once during the whole game. He was continually pacing, and jumping and spinning and calling out plays and yelling things. I couldn't be completely sure, but I figured he'd covered more ground than anybody who was actually playing in the game.

When I wasn't on the court, I had kept one eye on the game and the other on Coach. I knew he was trying to be more low-key and relaxed, but *trying* and *doing* were two very different things.

A couple of times, when somebody on the team made a mistake, he yelled out something — once it was at me. But most of the time he reacted to a bad play by doing a little dance and turning his back to the court — sort of like if it was too painful to even watch.

As well, he'd said a couple of things to the ref, and although he wasn't tossed, or even warned, I knew he was pushing where he probably shouldn't go. Maybe you could get the next call by yelling out something, or maybe you just got the ref mad at you and your team. Then you were in trouble. I'd seen refs take something a coach yelled and make sure that that team didn't get one call their way for the rest of the game.

All in all, he'd done pretty well. Then again, it wasn't that difficult to be easygoing when your team had been up from the first whistle and had never looked back.

"Nick, Kia, get ready for a change," Coach said.

"Sure," I said as I got to my feet and started to pull off my warm-up shirt. Normally I would have been excited to get back on — who likes being on the bench? — but I today I would have been happy to just stay off.

I'd played about the same number of minutes as I usually did, but I felt like my legs didn't quite have the same amount of "go" in them. I'd never played for a team that ran a full press and man to man for an entire game. Heck, I'd never even *heard* of a team doing that. It had obviously worn down the other team, but it had also had an effect on us as well. We could get through this game, but we still had three more to play today.

Kia and I went and kneeled down by the scorer's table, ready for Coach to call for subs.

"We've done pretty good," Kia said.

"Not bad. How you feeling?"

"Okay ... tired," Kia answered.

"Me too. I was wondering if we're going to have anything left for the next game, or the one after that, or the last game."

"I was wondering about that too. Do you think there'll be any gas left in our tanks for the last game?"

"I guess we'll see," I said. "Either way, at least we didn't lose all our games."

"What do you mean lose them all?"

I paused. If I were talking to anybody except Kia, I wouldn't have gone any further.

"These teams are the best," I said. "Weren't

you at least a little nervous that we wouldn't be able to compete with them?"

Kia didn't answer.

"Weren't you?" I asked again.

She shrugged. "A little, but what I *was* thinking isn't as important as what I *am* thinking now."

"And that is?" I asked.

"That maybe we're not as good as all the teams in this tournament, but we're sure better than at least one other team."

"A lot better," I agreed.

"So you know what that makes me think?" she asked.

"I know," I said. "Maybe we're better than more than one other team. Maybe more than a lot of teams."

Kia smiled. "Maybe better than all the other teams."

"You mean in our pool?" I asked.

"Maybe in the whole tournament. What do you think?" she asked.

"I think that we're going to find out soon enough."

I practically stumbled into the room, pushed and propelled by everybody else shoving in behind me. I felt exhausted, drained, beat . . . and happy. We'd pulled off four straight wins and made it through to the next round! I flopped down on the bed.

"No time for showers!" my father called out. "We're meeting downstairs in fifteen minutes for a late supper. Just get changed."

Tristan, David, Jamie and Mark went into the other room while Kia grabbed her bag.

"Getting changed doesn't mean wearing a dress, right?" she asked.

My father laughed. "No dress . . . unless you want to wear one."

"Not likely," she scoffed, and took her bag into the bathroom and closed the door.

My father flopped down on the bed beside me. "You played well. You all played well."

"Thanks," I said.

"I was a little worried during that last game, though," my father said.

"It was close," I agreed.

"I wasn't worried about the score," he said. "I thought Len was going to get tossed."

I was more than a little worried about that as well. With each passing game he'd become more vocal. He'd argued a couple of calls and the ref had come over and given him a warning.

"He's trying to control himself, but I think it's getting harder as the games get more serious," my father said.

"I thought all the games were serious."

"They are, but each one gets more serious. You've reached the quarterfinals. You win that one and you reach the semis. Win that one and you're in the finals. It doesn't get more serious than that."

"What would happen if he had gotten tossed?" I asked.

"I'm listed on the roster as the assistant coach, so I guess I'd take over."

"You?"

"Don't sound so shocked. It's not like I don't know a thing or two about basketball."

"I know, it's just you haven't coached me for years, since I played house league."

"It has been a while, but the game's basically the same whether it's house league, rep ball, college or even the NBA. You just — "

"Guys, come quick!" David yelled as he raced into the room.

My father and I both jumped off the bed.

"What's wrong?" my father questioned.

"Nothing! Nothing's wrong! We're on TV!"

We both skidded into the room in time to see Coach being interviewed by that reporter.

"Get the other guys!" Jamie yelled, and Tristan flew out of the room. A few seconds later I heard him pounding on the door and yelling for them.

"Turn it up!" Kia yelled as she ran into the room as well. She was followed in almost immediately by Tristan, and then the rest of the team barreled in, pushing and shoving and yelling.

"Be quiet!" my father yelled, and the noise dropped off, although everybody continued to jockey for position in front of the TV.

"There is probably no youth tournament in the entire country that is as prestigious as the annual Mumford International Invitational Tournament. To be here a team has to be special," the reporter said, staring directly into the camera.

"That's us, we're special!" Tristan agreed loudly.

"But of all the special teams, one may stand out more than any of the others," she continued.

"That's right, she's seen us play!" Al added.

"Look, there I am! I'm on TV!" L.B. yelled.

"Where are you? I don't see you!" I questioned.

"Are you blind? I'm right there in the background, behind . . . okay, I'm gone now," he said as he ran out of the picture behind the reporter.

"And what are the things that make this team special?" the reporter asked. "Let's begin with their coach, Len Barkley, one of the most successful college players of all time."

The screen changed to a shot of Coach being interviewed by the reporter, and then some footage of him on the sidelines during one of our games today.

"There's everybody!" David screamed.

It was a shot of all of us surrounding Coach

during a time-out. The screen then changed back to a shot of just the reporter holding a microphone.

"And those who remember Len Barkley from his playing days must surely remember the accident that ended his career and stopped him from pursuing greatness in the NBA."

I had a terrible feeling that I knew what was going to come next. Grainy black-and-white images of basketball players wearing funny-looking old-fashioned uniforms and strange haircuts flashed across the screen, and then a ball flew loose and – I couldn't bear to look. I turned to L.B. and watched as he cringed at the sight of his father getting hurt.

"A career ended because of one frightening injury – an injury that still makes me want to look away," the reporter said. It was nice to know I wasn't the only one.

"But here we are years later, watching as Len Barkley the player has become *Coach* Barkley to a team of kids entered in the tournament. And, if his four straight wins today are any indication, he has that same magic as a coach that he had as a player."

"That's us, we're the magic!" Tristan shouted out.

"Instrumental in his success thus far is Coach Barkley's secret weapon," she said.

"We have a secret weapon?" I questioned.

"And that secret weapon is named Kia," she continued.

"Kia?" a bunch of people all repeated at once as the TV was filled with the image of Kia, wearing her fancy dress and high-heeled sandals, standing up on the stage.

"Looking at this pretty young girl," the reporter said, "you would never suspect that she is not only a basketball player, but is leading her team to victory!"

The screen image changed to show Kia, in her uniform, on the court. It showed her taking a lay-up during the warm-ups. Then it rapidly changed to her covering a man — I think it was our second game — and then taking a shot, and then making a pass.

"Whether it's taking charge on defense, feeding a teammate or making the buckets herself, young Kia is showing the boys the way the game should be played as she leads her team to victory after victory. We'll continue to follow Kia and her team as they continue their quest for gold. This is Elyse Parris reporting from the Mumford International Invitational Basketball Tournament!"

The screen image changed back to two guys sitting behind a desk, and one of them had started to say something about the weather when Coach reached over and clicked the TV off. I hadn't even realized he was in the room.

"Kia isn't our leader," Tristan protested. "I got more court time today than she did!"

"And I got the most rebounds for sure!" Jordan added.

"And I got twenty-three assists in the games so nobody — "

"All of you stop!" Coach bellowed, and the room fell silent. "Everybody sit down."

There were only two chairs and they were taken. A couple of guys sat on the end of one of the beds.

"Now!" Coach yelled. "Everybody sit down now!"

I practically dropped to the floor. Coach scowled and started pacing around the room.

"*I* got the most points. *I* got the most rebounds. *I* got the most court time. There's no place for any of this talk. There isn't, and never will be, an '*I*' in '*team*.'"

"But there is an 'I' in Kia," L.B. said under his breath.

Coach shot him a dirty look.

"This is exactly what I thought would happen," Coach said. "Some reporter making a story up and it distracts us from our goal. Does anybody here think Kia went looking for this story?"

"She didn't even want to be interviewed," I said, defending my best friend.

"Exactly!" Coach said. "Kia is a leader on this team, just like every one of you is a leader. There are going to be games we can't win without her and games we're going to lose because of her. Just like with everybody else. We're a team and we're going to be acting like a team. Does everybody understand?"

Everybody voiced agreement or nodded their heads.

"Good. We played as a team and now we're going to get dressed and eat supper as a team." He paused. "And after that . . . we're going to have some fun as a team."

Chapter Twelve

The whole video arcade was packed with kids. It looked like half the teams in the tournament were in here. It was hard to get close enough to even see a game being played, so actually playing one was a long shot. My father and Coach sat out on a bench in the lobby right in front of the arcade. They'd come in for a couple of minutes and complained about the heat and crowd and noise. This was one time I really didn't disagree. The noise from all the games was incredible. Even worse was the heat. The combination of all those video machines and the bodies packed together like little sardines made it so hot I was sweating more than I did during the games.

We'd run into some of the kids from teams

that we'd played that day. It was so crowded that it was impossible not to bump into people. A few had nodded their heads and a couple had even talked to us — mainly about the news report. It seemed like there were a whole lot of people who'd caught it on TV. A couple of times I'd heard somebody say something about our "secret weapon" as we passed by.

Kia had stayed right by me since we left the room. I was used to her being close — after all, she was my best friend. What I wasn't used to was her not saying much of anything. She nodded her head or mumbled a few words when I asked her something, but she really wasn't talking. That was so un-Kialike.

"Look," Tristan said. "There's the New York team."

I'd already noticed them and moved in the other direction. "I wonder how they did today?" I asked.

"Only one way to find out," Tristan said. "Let's ask them."

"Do you think that — " I stopped talking, since Tristan had already turned and walked toward them. Reluctantly I followed, and Kia trailed behind me.

"Hey, New York!" Tristan yelled over the noise. "How'd you do today?"

"We won our division," one of them said.

"As expected," another said. "And you?"

"No problem," Tristan said. "Not even a contest."

"*You* won your division?" one of them questioned.

"You sound surprised," Kia said, sounding annoyed.

"Maybe I should be surprised that *your* team won their division."

"It would be a surprise — no, a shock — if we didn't win!"

"He's right," Tristan said, jumping in.

Why was he defending these guys?

"I bet everybody here at this whole tournament figures you're the team to beat," Tristan said.

"You got that right!" one of their players said.

"Bank on it!" another trumpeted.

"And not just the division, but the whole tournament. You're supposed to win, aren't you?" Tristan continued.

"No more truer words were ever spoken," another New York player agreed.

"So if you win, then you're just doing what's expected, right?" Tristan said.

"Of course."

"And if you lose, it would be a real disappointment, like choking big time, right?" Tristan looked over and winked at me. Now I knew what he was doing: he was trying to psych them out.

"Well . . . I guess so . . . "

"Wow," Tristan said. "That means that unless you win, everybody will look at you all and think you're nothing but a bunch of big choke artists, especially all the other players from the New York teams that won before."

"My brother was on the team two years ago," one of the New York players said. "He'll never let me hear the end of it . . . never."

"Just think, if you reach the finals and lose, then you'll still be just a bunch of losers. Nothing less than winning everything will be good enough," Kia said. She'd obviously figured out what Tristan was doing.

"And you'd go home and everybody, I mean everybody, would be so disappointed in you, or mad, or make fun of you. That would be hard. I don't envy you guys," Tristan said.

"Not like us," I added. "We've already done better than people thought we would. We're already winners no matter what happens."

"And you guys," Kia said, "are losers unless you win the whole thing. Talk about pressure. We better get going now."

The three of us turned and walked away, trying hard to stop from giggling.

"That was fun," I yelled to Kia and Tristan.

They nodded in agreement.

"It's the only fun we've had in here," Kia said.

"It's too hot," Tristan added.

"And I haven't even been able to play a game yet," I continued.

"Maybe we should go for a swim now," Kia suggested.

"Swim?"

"In the pool. Since everybody in the world is in here, the pool must be practically empty," Kia reasoned.

"Do you think Coach will let us?" I asked.

"He said we could go in as long as we didn't swim . . . you know, just for a dip. How about me and Tristan round up the guys and you go and ask?"

"Why me?"

"Why not you? Besides, I think it's better we get out of here before the New York team realizes what we did to them," Kia said.

She had a point there. I started off through the arcade, weaving my way through the crush of kids. It was impossible to move without bumping into or brushing by people. I pushed open the glass door and was hit by a rush of cool, quiet air. The door swung shut, sealing in the sounds. I took a deep breath of air. It felt good in my lungs.

My father and Coach were just up ahead. Standing with them were a few other men, including the mayor.

"That isn't right!" Coach suddenly bellowed as he jumped to his feet.

I froze in my tracks.

"We're playing by them! You show me one place in the rules where it says that this is — " He stopped mid-sentence as he saw me standing there, watching. He motioned for me to come.

"Hi, Nicky," my father said.

"How long have you been standing there?" Coach asked.

"I just came out of the arcade . . . just now."

"Maybe you should go back inside and join the rest of the guys . . . um, players," Coach said.

I went to go and then stopped. "We were thinking it was too crowded in there and too hot. We wanted to go for a swim — I mean, a dip in the pool . . . if that's okay?"

"The pool?" Coach asked, as if he didn't understand the word.

"The outdoor pool. You said we could if we just soaked and didn't swim. We'd just go for a while," I suggested.

"It would give us a chance to continue our discussion," the mayor said to him.

"I could go with them," my father suggested.

"It might be better if you come with me," Coach said.

"There's a lifeguard, and you could join them

right after we're through," one of the men said. He looked familiar, and then I realized he'd been up on the stage at the big table. He was one of the officials of the tournament.

Coach didn't answer right away. He looked like he was thinking.

"I guess that would be all right, for just a while. What I need, then, is for the whole team to go and everybody to stay together," Coach said.

"And it won't be for long," my father added.

"Sure, we'll just go for a while," I agreed.

"We'll meet you down there shortly," Coach said. "And Nick . . . you're in charge."

"No problem. Kia and Tristan are rounding everybody up now," I said, and turned to go.

"Nick!" my father called out.

He walked toward me. "I don't want you talking to anybody about what you just heard."

"I didn't hear anything."

He cocked one eyebrow at me.

"I didn't hear *enough* to understand what's going on. What is going on?"

"Nothing that you need to worry about. There's just a little disagreement about rules and eligibility."

I nodded my head, although I had absolutely no idea what he meant.

"And Nick, keep an extra eye on Kia."

*

Everybody had thought the pool was a great idea. We'd gotten out of the arcade, up to our rooms and into our suits in record time. Approaching the pool, it was apparent that it was practically deserted. There were some older people and a couple of families with small children, but nobody else.

"Group cannonball!" Jamie screamed.

Almost all at once people dropped their towels, kicked off their flip-flops and pulled off T-shirts, scrambling to the side of the pool. We all got there at almost the same instant.

"One . . . two . . . three . . . jump!" Jamie yelled, and we all threw ourselves into the air.

I splashed down, breaking the surface and plunging underwater! It felt fantastic! I bobbed up to the surface and saw choppy waves bouncing back and forth across the surface of the pool. Across the way, on her tower, the lifeguard jumped to her feet. She looked like she wasn't happy, but didn't say a word.

I took a few strokes back toward the side of the pool. Looking up I saw Kia standing there – she hadn't jumped in with the rest of us.

"Hey, Kia!" Tristan yelled. Obviously I wasn't the only one who'd noticed. "Come on in, the water's great!"

"Maybe she doesn't want to get her hair wet,"

somebody suggested.

"Yeah, you can never tell when you might end up on camera again and you have to look your best!" L.B. laughed.

I cringed. I expected Kia to say something. Instead she turned and started to walk away. What was she doing?

"Come, on, Kia, I was just joking," L.B. yelled out.

I quickly pulled myself out of the pool and started after her. I looked back. L.B. was doing the same thing. I knew he hadn't meant anything mean – he wasn't a mean guy. I raced after her, L.B. right behind me.

"Kia, wait up!" I yelled.

She turned and stopped at the end of the pool.

"The water's really nice and it was your idea to go into the pool to begin with, so you can't just leave!" I pleaded.

"Who's leaving?" she asked.

"I was just joking around; come on in the pool," L.B. said.

"I am going in," Kia said. "I just thought I'd go in a different way."

"Different?" I asked.

She placed one hand on the ladder leading up to the two high diving boards and then smiled.

"You don't mean . . . ?"

Her smile widened, she kicked off her flip-flops and then started up the ladder. I stood at the bottom, looking up as she took step after step. There were two boards, one partway up, and a second right at the very top. Jumping from the low one would take a lot of guts. Going to the very top would be like jumping from an airplane. It had to be twenty feet high. I was sure she'd just go to the lower one.

Kia reached the landing at the first board. She stopped and looked around. She looked down at me and then started out for the board.

"Be careful!" I yelled up.

She slowly walked out onto the board. It bounced with each step she took. Carefully she made her way to the very end of the board. It dipped slightly under her weight. She gazed down at the water beneath her.

I noticed that the sound of the guys splashing and fooling around had stopped. I looked over at them. They were all staring at Kia. Actually, everybody in or around the pool was looking at her. The lifeguard was still in her chair, but her eyes were focused on the tower.

"You can do it, Kia!" Jamie called out.

I felt like yelling up, "You don't have to do it," but I kept my mouth shut. I knew there was no point in even trying to talk Kia out of, or into, anything. Once she'd decided on doing something, there was no use in trying to confuse her with reason, logic or the facts. At least she'd chosen the lower board.

Kia bounced at the end of the board, and it dipped dangerously.

"Come on, Kia . . . jump before you fall," I said under my breath.

"She can swim . . . right?" L.B. asked anxiously.

"Yeah, she's a good swimmer," I reassured him. "But I know she's never jumped off a diving board from that high up before."

"Look!" L.B. called out. "She's coming down!"

Kia had turned and walked off the board. She was coming back down and – she wasn't coming back! She had reached the ladder and started up for the high board!

"Kia, what are you doing?" I yelled up.

"Figure it out," she called back down.

Without thinking, I grabbed onto the ladder and started up after her. Maybe if I talked to her I could convince her that she . . . who was I fooling? Then again, maybe I could tell her that Coach had told me we could go swimming, but that he also told me nobody should go off the tower. She'd believe that, wouldn't she?

I doubled my pace up the tower, reaching the first landing before Kia had reached the top of the second. Man, did I hate heights. I grabbed onto the railing and, holding on firmly, started up the next flight.

"Kia! You can't do this," I puffed as I reached the top landing. "Coach said you can't!"

Kia threw me a look of disbelief. "Coach isn't here and he really didn't say anything about the tower, right?"

"Well . . . "

"I can always tell when you're lying," she said.

"And I can always tell when you're going to do something stupid," I snapped back.

"I'm not doing anything stupid. I'm just jumping in the pool. Coach said we were allowed to jump into the pool."

"This isn't what he meant and you know it!"

"I guess since he's not here, the only way we'll find out if I'm wrong is if somebody tells him. Are you going to tell?"

"You know I wouldn't do that. Nobody on the team will if you don't want them to."

"Then I'm going to jump." She paused. "Did you come up here to jump too?"

"Of course not!"

"Too bad, because boy are you going to look like a big chicken when I jump and you crawl back down the ladder."

I shook my head in disbelief. Did she really think she could get me to do this by calling me a chicken?

Kia walked off the platform and onto the board.

It bounced slightly under her feet as she slowly and deliberately moved farther out. She looked over the side at the water below. I held onto the railing with one hand and looked down. We were a long way up – a long way.

"Kia, can you just explain to me why you're doing this?" I asked.

"I'm going for a dip in the pool, like I suggested when we first drove by the pool yesterday."

"You know what I mean. Is it because of people kidding you about the TV news thing?" I asked.

She shook her head.

"Then what?" I asked.

"Because I want to," she said.

Kia turned around, walked to the very end of the board, bounced twice and jumped!

I gasped in disbelief at her sudden disappearance, which was followed by a loud splash and a cheer from everybody watching. I leaned out even farther. I was just in time to see her come back up to the surface, wave to the crowd and then swim to the side. Thank goodness she was okay.

"Your turn next, Nick!" Tristan yelled up.

"Come on, Nick, you can do it!" Jamie screamed.

"Do a cannonball!" Jordan called out.

I watched as Kia climbed out of the pool to join everybody else on the deck. People slapped her on the back. I felt very alone, very exposed, standing by myself up on the tower while everybody else was so very far below me.

"Jump!" L.B. screamed.

"It won't kill you," Kia called out. "At least it didn't kill me! Don't be afraid."

I was going to yell back something about not being afraid, but actually I was.

"What are you waiting for?" David asked.

What was I waiting for? I either jumped or turned around and started to climb down. Instead I stood frozen to the spot. My feet didn't want to move, but my mind was racing, trying to figure a way out of it and — I smiled to myself.

"I'm waiting for the rest of you!" I called out.

There was no answer from below.

"We're a team . . . remember? I'm not jumping until the rest of you come up here too!"

No way they were all going to come up here, and if they didn't come up then I'd have an excuse to climb down.

"Teams do everything together!" I called out.

Now it was their turn to be frozen. Nobody moved. Nobody said a word. I'd wait a few more seconds and then I'd climb down.

"I'm coming right up!" Tristan yelled back.

He started running toward the tower, and like a floodgate being opened the rest of the team came running after him.

A loud whistle screamed out. "No running on the deck!" yelled the lifeguard.

Either they didn't hear her or didn't care, because they kept running to the tower. Within seconds I felt the vibrations coming up the tower as they started to climb up the stairs beneath me. Within seconds Tristan appeared on the platform, followed by Jamie and David and Al and the top half of Jordan.

"Is everybody coming?" I asked in disbelief.

"Everybody," Tristan answered. "Go ahead, jump."

There were now eleven bodies on the ladder below me. There was only one way off this tower. Boy, was this stupid. Boy, was I stupid. I walked to the end, bounced once and flung myself off.

Chapter Thirteen

"You have to get to sleep, Nick," my father whispered as he bent down beside me. He'd been over in the corner of the room, reading by a small light.

"I've been trying," I whispered back.

"It's a big day tomorrow and you need to be rested."

"I know. Is everybody else asleep?" I asked, even though I was pretty sure I already knew the answer. I hadn't heard a sound from anybody.

"They all dropped off immediately. It was a pretty long day. Aren't you tired?"

"My body's tired," I admitted.

Between the games and the swimming and all the excitement, I really was tired.

"Can't shut off your mind, right?" he asked.

I nodded my head.

"Thinking about today's games and wondering about tomorrow's?" my father asked.

Again I nodded. That was certainly part of it. I was also thinking about our team "swim." It had been such an incredible rush to jump off the tower that we all did it again and again and again. I must have jumped five times. If swimming would weaken our legs, what would all that climbing up stairs do for them? It was the strangest thing, but, even though we were doing something we probably shouldn't be doing, it was the first time I'd felt like we were all together – all part of the same team. It felt good.

There was also another reason I couldn't sleep. I knew something was going on. Coach and my father hadn't come to the pool for a long time. Thank goodness nobody was on the tower when they showed up. And when they came, they huddled together and kept on talking and both had serious looks on their faces. I didn't know what, but something was wrong – something to do with the rules.

"Dad," I whispered, "what's eligibility?"

My father didn't answer.

"Dad?" I asked. "Did you hear me?"

"I was just thinking," he said. "You don't know what eligibility means either?" I asked.

Again he chuckled. "Eligibility means that you are allowed to do something or be somewhere. The question is whether I should I talk to you about it."

"What do you mean?" I asked.

"Maybe it would be best if I left it to Len to talk to your whole team together."

I sat up in bed. "Do you mean we're not allowed to play?"

Again my father didn't answer right away. "It's not the whole team and it's not definite. Nothing's being decided until tomorrow . . . probably after our quarterfinal game."

"So maybe we can't even play?"

"You can play, Nick. Most of you can play no matter what they decide."

"Most of us?" I asked.

"All of you, except for one player."

"Who? Who can't play?"

"Nick, it isn't definite yet, and I've already said more than I should have." He paused. "This isn't exactly the best thing to do to help you get to sleep, is it?"

It was my turn to chuckle. "Not exactly."

"Nothing's going to be decided tonight, so there's nothing you can do about it. Just go to sleep."

"But — "

"No buts," he said softly. "Just roll over and

close your eyes and get to sleep. Okay?"

"I'll try," I answered, and tried to snuggle down into the covers. There was no way I was going to get to sleep now for a long time. It didn't help that I could hear Kia gently snoring away in the bed next to me. She could sleep through a hurricane. And she complained about me being too loud! I wondered which player it was. It had to be one of the new players, because the rest of us had played rep before and nobody ever complained about us not being eligible.

"Dad?"

There was a deep sigh. "Yes, Nick?"

"It isn't me, is it?"

"You?"

"I'm not the one who's not supposed to play, am I?"

"Of course not, Nick. Why would you even think that?"

"I don't know . . . I just worry sometimes."

There was silence.

"Dad . . . it's one of the new players, isn't it?"

My question was greeted by silence.

"Dad?"

"Nick . . . we'll do the best we can . . . just have faith that your coach and I will take care of things. Can you do that?"

"I can try," I said. But trying to believe wasn't going to get me any closer to sleeping tonight.

I put up another shot. Air ball — again. The floor was the only thing I'd managed to hit in the entire warm-up.

"You're going to have some fantastic game," Coach said as he tossed me my ball.

"I am?" I asked in disbelief.

"Sure. That is, if you believe in that old myth that a bad warm-up means a good game. Because if you do believe that, then you're going to have the very best game of your entire life."

"Sorry," I mumbled. "I'm trying."

"Probably too hard. Everybody's trying too hard. The whole team looks tired," Coach said. "I guess four games in one day was pretty hard."

Not to mention the trips up the tower at the pool – and believe me, nobody was going to mention it.

Coach walked over to the bench, then blew his whistle really loud, the sound cutting through all the other noise in the gym.

"Everybody come on in!" he yelled.

We all grabbed our balls and started for the bench. "Why does he want us in?" Kia asked. "We're not through with our warm-ups."

I had a sinking feeling that maybe he was going to tell us about somebody not being able to play.

"Gather around me," Coach said.

We all sat down on the floor.

"You know that there were forty teams entered in this tournament. Forty. Forty very good teams. And now? There are only eight teams left. Thirty-two have packed their bags and are on their way home. You have to be incredibly proud of yourselves for getting this far. I know I'm certainly proud of you."

It was nice of him to say that. Was this his way of softening the blow when he told somebody that it was all over?

"And if we lose today, we can leave here with our heads held high. We did our best," he continued. "I couldn't help but notice that you all seem tight, nervous, not your usual selves."

Other members of the team nodded in agreement. I'd been so busy thinking that I hadn't even noticed how anybody else was doing.

"This has to be the biggest crowd any of you have ever played before," he said.

I looked over at the bleachers. They looked to be about a quarter filled, and I'd been told that capacity was around six thousand, so that meant there were close to fifteen hundred people here.

"Not to mention the cameras, and, of course, our good friend, Ms. Parris," Coach continued.

She'd tried to talk to us when we came in. Coach

told her to leave us all alone. She was getting more pushy and Coach was getting less polite.

"Just try to forget all about them. Forget all about all the people in the stands. Just think about playing some ball and having some fun. Win or lose, life goes on. Understand?"

"Sure, Coach," Kia said. "But if it's all the same with you, I'd rather we go on with life after *winning*."

Coach's face broke into a gigantic grin and he started to laugh. "I couldn't have said it better myself. Everybody take a couple more shots while I figure out our starting line-up."

"Time out!" Coach screamed. "Time out!"

I wanted to run to the sidelines, but I felt like I had nothing left to give. It didn't really matter, though. There was less than three seconds to go and we were down by two. There wasn't enough time to get the ball down court for a shot. We'd come back from being fifteen points down at the half, fighting and scrapping and getting this close. Unfortunately, close wasn't good enough.

"Okay, everybody, listen up," Coach said. "We have one last chance."

I felt like saying not much of a chance, but I didn't say anything.

"I want Jordan, L.B. and Kia to go to the hoop,

be right under the net. Mark, you stay right out at the top of the key. Nick, you're putting the ball in."

"I don't know if I can throw it that far," I said, looking down at the far net.

"You don't have to *throw* it at all."

"But I don't understand."

"I don't want you to throw the ball. I want you to roll it."

"Roll it?" I questioned.

"Like a bowling ball, right to Mark."

"But why am I doing that?"

"For three reasons. First, I know you can't throw it that far – nobody on the team can. Second, they're not expecting us to roll the ball. And third, because the clock doesn't start until somebody touches the ball. You roll it down the court, Mark picks it up and puts up a shot. Simple," he said, and shrugged. "And Mark, remember you have virtually no time. Just grab the ball, spin and shoot. If it goes in you're a hero. If you miss we all understand you did your best."

Mark nodded. His face was so serious and solemn. Mark had been my friend long enough for me to know that if he did miss, he'd blame himself, even if nobody else did.

"Get in position," Coach said.

We started out. As I moved beside the ref I looked over and saw Coach bending over right beside the timer, saying something right into his ear. Of course I figured he was reminding — or warning — him about how he better not start the clock until the ball reached Mark.

The other team broke out of its huddle. They'd already started to celebrate the victory. I hated when teams did that. The only thing worse than a bad loser was a bad winner. One of their men – the man covering the throw-in – sauntered up to stand right in front of me.

"Why even bother?" he said. "This one is in the books. We win and your team goes home."

He was right. This was almost impossible, but still . . . there was a chance.

"You're going to feel awfully stupid when we make this shot."

There was something about the way I'd said what I said that took away that smug look on his face for a split second. "Yeah, right," he said, and the look of confidence returned to his face. "Like I'm *really* afraid."

The ref handed me the ball and started counting off the time. Everybody was where they were supposed to be. All I had to do was make the throw . . . I mean, the roll. I stepped slightly to the side to avoid the man covering the throw-in. I reared back and heaved the ball with all my might. It bounced and skittered and skimmed across the floor, finally rolling . . . straight to-

ward Mark! His man was well off under the net, expecting some sort of long bomb to our players under the net. Then, catching a glimpse of the ball coming, everybody broke out toward the ball. Mark stepped out to reach the ball first. He was just outside the three-point line. He grabbed the ball and all in one motion spun around and shot and the buzzer sounded and the ball went up and up and hit the rim and spun around and dropped! I looked for the ref — he signaled that the basket counted, and counted as a three-pointer! We'd won! We'd won!

I screamed and ran the length of the court, reaching Mark at almost the same instant that everybody else on the court and from the bench reached him. We all tumbled over in a massive pile of arms, legs, knees and elbows!

Chapter Fourteen

I finally managed to unscramble myself from the pile. I looked around. The two coaches from the other team were arguing with the refs. From this distance, over the noise of the crowd, I couldn't hear anything, but I could tell by their expressions and gestures that they were very angry. It also didn't take a genius to figure out what they were arguing about — they must have been saying that the shot didn't count, that it was still in Mark's hands at the buzzer.

The refs seemed to be holding their own in the arguing department. Finally, the two refs shook their heads, turned away and the two coaches stormed angrily away – obviously unhappy with the result.

I wanted to just ask Coach to make sure that we'd won and that was the end of it and . . . Coach and my father were standing by our bench along with three men wearing tournament-official shirts. I recognized the mayor, but not the other two. Coach was jumping up and down. I stopped in my tracks, afraid to go any closer. I'd seen him upset — heck, I'd seen him down-right lose it, he was so angry — but that was nothing compared to what he looked like right now. Why was he so angry? Had they told him that we'd lost the game? And, if we'd lost, then why weren't the coaches from the other team happy? Both teams couldn't have lost.

The three officials started to walk away. My father was holding Coach by the arms, physically stopping him from going after them. My father half pushed, half dragged Coach toward the dressing-room door, and the two of them disappeared through the door.

None of this made any sense at all. What was happening? I looked over at the other team's bench. The kids were just sitting there with their heads in their hands. A couple of them looked like they were in tears. One of their coaches was stomping around like an elephant. I looked up at the scoreboard. The score still stood – we'd won by one point. We had to have won.

I ran down the floor to where everybody else

was still celebrating, completely oblivious to whatever was happening.

"Kia!" I screamed. "We have to get to the dressing room!"

"We have to celebrate!" she shouted, bouncing up and down.

"Something's wrong!" I yelled, and not only Kia, but Mark and David and Jamie as well stopped cheering and looked at me.

"What do you mean?" Jamie demanded.

"I don't know," I said, shaking my head. "We have to ask Coach. We have to go to the dressing room."

Everybody grabbed somebody else and got their attention. The whole team trailed after me across the floor. I pushed open the dressing-room door. I expected to hear yelling, but the only noise was coming from the people behind me. Coach was sitting on a bench. My father was standing right beside him. They both looked up as we entered. Coach didn't look angry. Worse – he looked sad.

Everybody stopped talking and, without being asked, sat down on the bench across from Coach. Silently we waited. And waited. Finally Coach spoke.

"I'm not exactly sure where to begin."

"We won the game . . . right?" Tristan asked.

Coach nodded. "But that's not the issue."

"Then what?" L.B. asked.

Coach didn't answer right away. I could see him thinking through his words before he spoke.

"We were told that there was going to be a meeting this morning by tournament officials," he began. "And they met and have decided that we have been playing with an ineligible player."

"A what?" Jordan asked.

"A player who isn't supposed to be playing in this tournament," I answered.

"You mean like somebody who's too old?" he asked.

"We're all the right age," Jamie protested. "Aren't we?"

Again Coach nodded. "It isn't the age of our players that's being questioned. It's a matter of gender."

"What's gender?" L.B. asked.

"Kia," Coach said quietly. "They're saying that Kia can't play because she's a girl."

"But there was another girl who competed!" I exclaimed. "Your sister . . . thirty years ago!"

"She competed in the first two rounds. Before the championship game we were told that she couldn't play or we'd forfeit the game," Coach said.

"And?" L.B. asked.

"And she didn't play."

"But that was thirty years ago," I argued.

"Even more," my father agreed.

"So that was in the olden days. Things have to be different now!"

"That's what I thought, Nick. That's why I didn't think there could be any problem with Kia playing. It wasn't like I made a secret of her being a girl. Just think about how she was dressed at the reception."

"No mistaking her for a boy, for sure," I agreed.

"She's got to play. There has to be something that we can do!" Tristan protested.

"There's an appeal process. We can put our case before the final appeal board," my father explained.

"And we're going to do that," Coach confirmed. "There's just one problem. The board doesn't meet until *after* we play our semifinal game."

"How is that a problem?" L.B. asked.

"Well, if we play Kia in that game, after being officially told that she's ineligible, and we lose the appeal, then the entire team is disqualified."

"And *that* is our problem," my father agreed.

"So, if she plays and we don't win the appeal, then everybody is kicked out. Is that what you're saying?" L.B. asked.

Both Coach and my father nodded in agreement.

Kia, who hadn't said a word or moved a muscle

during the entire discussion, slowly got to her feet.

"There isn't any problem," she said. It was obvious that she was fighting back tears. "There's no problem because I'm not going to play."

Kia turned around and ran out of the room, leaving us all there too stunned to say a word. I jumped to my feet and took a few steps after her.

"Nick!" my father said as he quickly got to his feet, "you stay here and I'll go after her!" He ran out the door right behind Kia, leaving the rest of us behind in stunned silence.

"So . . . " L.B. said. "You're saying that Kia can't play in the next game . . . right?"

"I'm not saying that," Coach said. "The tournament officials are saying that."

"But you said she could play as long as we won the appeal," I said.

"That's right. And if she plays in this game and we lose the appeal, the whole team is eliminated."

"You mean that even if we win the game none of us would play in the finals?" Jamie asked.

There was silence. It was obvious that everybody was taking this seriously.

"Coach," Tristan asked. "Do you think we can win that appeal thing?"

"I don't know."

"Do you think we can win the game without Kia playing?" L.B. asked.

"I don't know that either," he admitted.

"So what are you going to do? Is Kia going to play?" L.B. asked.

"Me? It's not my decision," he said.

"Then whose decision is it?" Tristan asked.

"Yours."

"Mine! It's my decision!" Tristan exclaimed.

"Not just you. The whole team."

"But you're the coach! You have to decide!"

He shook his head. "Thirty-four years ago they said my sister couldn't play and she didn't because the coach decided we couldn't fight against the ruling. And do you know what I did about it?" he asked.

Nobody answered.

"I did nothing. I knew it wasn't right, and I knew how bad it hurt my sister, but I didn't say a word. I just went out and played. I didn't act like her brother or like a teammate."

Coach got up from the bench. "You eleven decide whether your teammate plays or sits. I'll be waiting outside."

Chapter Fifteen

The noise of the door closing behind him was the only sound.

"He was joking . . . right?" Tristan asked.

"I don't think so," L.B. replied. "This isn't the sort of thing my father would joke about."

"So *we* have to decide if Kia should play?" David asked.

"It's our decision."

"Shouldn't we at least let Kia say what she thinks?" Jamie asked.

"That won't work," I said. "Kia won't play if she thinks there's even a chance it'll get the rest of us tossed out."

"Then maybe we should just do what she thinks and have her sit out," L.B. suggested. "It doesn't seem right that we should go against what Kia wants and risk all of us being kicked out."

"It's not what she wants," I argued. "She wants to play the game. She always wants to play. The only reason she said she didn't want to play is because of what might happen to the team if she does."

"That's right," Tristan said. "Kia's only thinking about what's best for the team."

Again everybody lapsed into silence. It was amazing to me how everything had changed so quickly from just a few minutes ago out on the court. Instead of jumping up and down excitedly, we all sat staring at the floor.

"We can't just sit here and do nothing," Jamie finally said. "The next game is in less than an hour."

"So what do you think we should do?" Jordan asked.

"Maybe we have to take a vote," he suggested.

"Yeah, a vote, that's a good idea!" David agreed.

"Do we need paper and pencils to make it like a secret ballot?" Mark asked.

"No, we can just raise our hands," I said. "There shouldn't be any secrets on a team."

"Okay," L.B. said. "We vote. There's eleven of us, so whatever six people vote for wins."

"No," I said. "We *all* have to agree. All of us have to vote one way or another."

"And if we can't agree?" L.B. asked.

"I don't know," I admitted. "But let's try to agree. All those who want Kia to play, even if it means we might get kicked out, raise your hand," I said as I put my hand into the air.

The crowd roared with approval once again as the third player on the other team's starting line-up was introduced. They screamed and yelled and cheered and stomped on the bleachers.

"Do you think they'll cheer that loud for us?" Mark asked.

"Not likely!" I snapped.

"I just wish somebody would have told us we were playing against the home team," Tristan said.

"It looks like everybody in Mumford is stuffed in here," I said.

The stands were completely packed, and there were more people lining up in the corridor and in the little spaces at the far ends of the bleachers. There didn't seem to be room for another person to squeeze in here. And of course the only people in the whole crowd I did know were the TV crew. The reporter, the cameraman and the other guy were set up in the far corner of the gym.

The crowd erupted again as the announcer introduced another member of the Mumford team.

"I was thinking," Tristan said. "The officials who said Kia couldn't play, they were from right here in this town, right?"

"I hadn't really thought about it, but I guess so," I admitted.

"And the people who are going to hear the appeal, they're probably from here too . . . right?"

"That would make sense."

"And this team and all the crowd are from here," Tristan continued.

"Of course."

The crowd erupted again as yet another hometown player was announced.

"You got a point in all this?" I asked.

"Well, I was just thinking. I don't figure it really matters one way or another whether we win or lose. Either way we *ain't* seeing the finals."

"I don't know," I argued. "You have to hope that people will be fair and — "

"And now I'd like to introduce the starting line-up of the Mississauga Magic!" the announcer thundered.

"Here we go," I said.

"Starting at forward," the announcer called out over the P.A. system, "wearing number three, is Kia Hartley!"

The crowd didn't cheer nearly as loudly. But that didn't stop the eleven of us from screaming at the top of *our* lungs.

"I don't know if we're going to play in the finals," I said to Tristan. "But I know we're going to win this game."

Tristan laughed. "Since when are you Mr. Confident?"

"Heck . . . look at who I've got as my teammates," I answered. "Do you think these guys — and girl — are going to lose?"

One by one the announcer called out the other four starters. I cheered just as loud for each of them. Part of me wanted to be a starter, but the other part was pretty happy to be right there on the bench for the first shift. It was all pretty intense, and it would calm me down just to watch for a couple of minutes.

Coach stood up and we all gathered around him.

"Before you go out there, I have a few words to say to all of you," Coach began. "I've played a lot of basketball in my life and I've been part of some very good teams, and a couple of great ones. And of all those teams, I've never been more proud of one than I am of this one. This is some team," he said, nodding his head slowly. "And whatever the score is at the end of this game . . . we walk away winners. Now go and play some ball."

*

"Foul, number four orange!" the ref shouted at

whistled down the play.

"...didn't touch him!" Tristan yelled. "He got ...ng but ball on that block!"

The ref turned away, ignoring him. "Two shots!"

Tristan was right: I hadn't touched their man. The game was less than five minutes old and that was the eighth foul called on our team – eight against us, and none against them.

We took to the line. His first shot hit the edge of the rim and bounced off to the side. Thank goodness they weren't very good from the foul line, or this game could have been getting out of sight. As it was, they were up by three. We were beating them from the field, but the foul shots they had made had put them in front.

"Time out!" Coach called out.

We trotted over to our bench and the ref trailed behind. "You want thirty seconds or a full time-out?" the ref asked.

"That's impressive," Coach snapped. "It's nice to see that you know at least one of the rules of the game. What sort of calls are you making out there?"

The ref's face hardened.

"I'll take a full time-out. Maybe you can use the time to go and read the rule book."

The ref turned away without saying a word.

"Call it for both teams or don't call it at all. Just because you live in Mumford doesn't mean you can't call an honest game!" Coach called after him.

That got the ref's attention. He spun around and started back toward our bench.

"Oh, good, it's nice to see you're at least awake!" Coach snapped.

"One more word and I'll give you a technical foul," the ref warned.

"Excellent!" Coach replied. "I'm so impressed that you know a second rule of basketball. Two down and another hundred or so to go!"

"That's a technical!" the ref yelled.

"Congratulations!" Coach thundered. "That's the first correct call you've made all night. Why don't you just pull a Mumford jersey on over top of your ref's shirt so there'll be no confusion about which team you want to win and — "

My father grabbed Coach by the arm and spun him around. "You have to stop," he hissed through closed teeth. "Just put it away for now. A second 't' and you're gone. He'll toss you from the game and then where will the team be?"

Coach looked like he was going to say something, but he didn't. Instead he sat down at the end of the bench.

The timer hit the buzzer to signal the end of the time-out.

"Okay, everybody, get out there and play!" my father yelled.

I sat on the end of the bench closest to the scorer's table. I looked up at the scoreboard. We were down by five points with just under three minutes left in the game. The game was over for me, though — I'd fouled out. I'd never done that before in my life. And I wasn't alone. Tristan was done. Jordan was done. Altogether we'd had thirty-one team fouls called against us. Thirty-one!

Mark dribbled down the court. He fed the ball inside to Al, who faked a drive and threw it back out to Mark. He put the shot up and it dropped for a three! I jumped off the bench. That brought us to within two points! Despite the thirty-one fouls, despite the other team having only been called for two, despite the fact they'd made twenty-five points from the foul line, we still weren't finished. We could pull this off . . . if the refs let us win. What a terrible thought – if the refs *let* us win.

I'd been around basketball all my life, and I'd hardly ever been to a game where somebody didn't think the refs were against one team – their team – and for the other. A couple of times I'd sort of believed it. This was the first time in my life I had no doubts. The calls on us got sillier and sillier. Even worse was the lack of calls against the Mumford team. I'd been hacked, slapped, grabbed and pushed all over the court without a single call. I'd heard about hometown reffing, but this was just ridiculous.

Coach was beside himself. He jumped and danced and screamed and questioned and a couple of times he tossed down the water bottle he was drinking. For the most part, the two refs just tried to ignore him. I thought they were so embarrassed about what they were doing that they didn't even have the nerve to look Coach in the eyes.

One of the refs blew his whistle. "Foul, number twelve orange!"

"You're right it was a foul!" Coach yelled. "A charging foul!"

The official at the scoring table pushed the buzzer.

"That's his fifth foul . . . he's gone."

David trotted over, his head down.

"That's okay, David, take a seat. And don't worry, it wasn't like that was a real foul!" Coach yelled, loud enough for everybody on the court, including the refs, to hear.

"Are you sending in another player?" one of the refs asked.

"What's the point?" Coach asked. "You're just going to make up calls to foul him out anyway."

"Jamie, go in," my father said, tapping him on the shoulder.

Jamie pulled off his warm-up shirt and ran

onto the court. The ref turned away and walked back toward the key. Everybody took up spots on the key for the free throw. The shot went up and clanked off the rim and to the side.

"Maybe you refs should take the shots for them as well!" Coach yelled.

"You have to be careful or he's going to toss you," my father warned Coach.

Coach shrugged.

The second shot went up the side and right down to where Al stood. He dribbled slightly out to the side and saw Kia breaking free. He fed the pass up and over her head. It bounced in front of her; she picked it up and started dribbling for the net! Nobody could get to her in time . . . if she made it the game would be all tied up!

She went up for the lay-up and bang, she got smashed from behind! The ball sailed up for the net while Kia crashed forward. The ball dropped through the hoop at the same time Kia crunched into the wall! Everybody on the bench jumped to their feet and screamed. Kia didn't get up, and the ref blew down the play.

Coach ran onto the court and Kia slowly sat up. He bent down and started talking to her and then offered her a hand and helped pull her to her feet. The whole crowd, which had become suddenly silent, started clapping. Slowly

Kia, Coach still holding her by the arm, came across the floor.

"Kia, are you okay?" I asked as I met her at the line.

"I'm fine . . . just a little shaken up."

"Coach," one of the refs asked, "are you calling a time-out?"

"Me calling a time-out?" Coach demanded. "You're supposed to call this one because of the injury."

"We're not calling a time-out," the ref said. "She either has to come back out or you have to substitute."

"And can the sub take the foul shot for her?" Coach asked.

"I didn't call a foul."

"What?" Coach yelled, leaping across the floor until he was practically on top of the ref. "You didn't call a foul on that! Are you completely blind? And even if you were blind you could have heard the collision! Do you think the wall jumped out to hit her?"

"That's enough from you. One more word and you're gone!" the ref snapped. "One more word!"

Coach turned his back to the ref, like he was going to stop. He was now facing my father. "If he tosses me, you're in charge."

"What do you mean I'm in charge?" my father asked, although we both knew what was coming up.

"Hey ref!" Coach called out, and the ref spun around and came stomping back toward us. "Can I ask you a question?"

The ref shrugged, but didn't say he couldn't.

"You been watching that camera over there?" Coach asked, pointing to the corner. The ref looked over.

"Because that camera was on that play and that girl has been their feature story, so I know they captured that last play on film. And you know what? When that goes out on the news, and I add my interview, you're going to look like the biggest, most incompetent, biased fool who ever *pretended* to ref a basketball game. So, think hard — and I know thinking isn't one of your strengths — are you sure you don't want to make a call on that play?"

The ref looked like he was angry enough to explode, or at the very least toss Coach right out of the gym. He looked over at the scorer's table. "One shot."

"Time out!" Coach yelled. "Full."

The rest of the team ran off the court while those of us on the bench rose to join them, surrounding Coach.

"Kia takes the shot. If she makes it, you put on the press. If she misses, you press. Either way, leave number sixteen open. I want them to send the ball to him. We want him to have the ball. Then foul him and foul him hard. If you can, smack his left wrist. He's left-handed and that might hurt his shooting. Now go and do it!"

They trotted out to the court. The rest of us stood on the sideline. There was no way I could sit down now.

Kia took the ball from the ref. I didn't know if Coach was bluffing when he said the camera had caught her being fouled, but now the camera was trained right at her.

Kia bent down slightly, dribbled the ball and put it up. It bounced off the rim, but Al grabbed the rebound and put it up. It dropped! We all screamed and yelled and jumped into the air.

"Press!" Coach yelled. "Press, press, press!"

Everybody except number sixteen was closely covered. The ball came in to him, and Jamie rushed over. He didn't even attempt to get the ball, instead smacking him as hard as he could.

Both refs blew their whistles and called out the foul. There was no arguing with that one.

"Double bonus, two shots!" one of them called out.

Everybody slowly walked down the court to our end.

Two shots. If he made both of them, the game was tied up. If he missed even one, we had the lead and ball with only twelve seconds left. All we'd have to do is hold on to the ball.

Number sixteen stood at the line. He bounced

the ball, and that was the only sound in the whole gym. The entire crowd had fallen silent. He bounced the ball again and then put up the shot – nothing but net. Darn. The crowd roared. If his wrist was hurting, it wasn't having any effect.

"The ball's in play after this shot!" the ref called out, and the crowd fell silent again.

He bounced the ball. He bounced it again. And again. What was he doing? Why was he taking so long.

"Come on, ref, he's only got five seconds!" Coach yelled. "Either he puts it up or you take it away!"

He put the ball up. It smashed into the bottom of the hoop and right into Al's hands again! Almost like an instant replay, he dribbled out and threw the ball up to Kia as she broke down the wing. She dribbled in and put the ball up, and it dropped just as the buzzer sounded! We all exploded as we rushed the court.

Chapter Sixteen

I had never seen that many people go so quiet. The entire crowd seemed to have had the wind knocked out of them and couldn't make a sound. Wordlessly they filed out of the gym. In the end, it hadn't mattered how loud the crowd had cheered during the game or even what the refs had done or not done. Despite it all we'd won.

Although I didn't really think it was going to make much difference. Winning on the court wasn't going to get us to the finals.

"We've got to get to the meeting so they can hear the appeal," my father said to me. "We need all of you to go back up to the rooms and wait for us and — "

"Why can't we come?" Kia asked.

"Yeah, we should be there," I agreed.

My father turned to Coach. "What do you think?"

"I think they have a point. It's about them, so it should include them."

We grabbed our things from behind the bench and stuffed them in our bags as we walked toward the door of the gym. Waiting there was the reporter.

"Congratulations, everybody! Finishes like that just keep making my story better and better!" she gushed. "Do you think that maybe I could have a few minutes to — "

"We don't have any time right now," Coach said as he kept walking. "I admire your persistence, but we have to go to a meeting."

"But you did promise me you'd let me interview everybody after the finals," she said.

Coach shook his head. "Sure, right after the finals."

"It'll be a great story if you win," she yelled after him as he continued to walk out of the gym.

"We can't win if we don't get to play in the finals," I mumbled as I passed by her.

"Of course you'll play in the finals," she said. "You won your game."

"But we still have to win the appeal," Kia explained.

"Appeal? What appeal? What are you talking about?' she asked.

"I thought reporters knew everything," Kia said.

"We only know what people tell us. Could you please explain?" she pleaded. "Why wouldn't you be playing in the finals?"

Kia quickly explained about her being disqualified because she was a girl and how the whole team could be kicked out if we didn't win the appeal.

"And that's happening right now?" the reporter asked.

"In a couple of minutes. That's where we're going," I explained.

"Good. Then all I have to do is follow right behind you and I'll be right there."

"You're going to the meeting?" I questioned.

She smiled. "This story just keeps getting better and better. I'd like to see somebody try to stop me."

We hurried out the door to catch up with everybody else, and the reporter, followed by her cameraman weighed down with his equipment, trailed behind us. The corridor was still packed with people exiting the game, and the going was very slow. A couple of times I lost sight of the heads of Coach and my father bobbing up and down in the crowd. Moving quickly, we caught up to them just as they walked through a door. We followed in behind them.

The room wasn't very big. There were desks and phones and a couple of bags filled with basketballs, and on the wall was a gigantic board listing all the games and scores. At the top of the board, each game leading up to the top of a pyramid, was the word "Finals", and the name of the New York Wild Cats was already waiting for the winner to be declared from our semifinal.

"We're here for the appeal," Coach said loudly.

Up at the front were the mayor and the two other men I recognized from the previous meetings. They all looked like they wanted to be someplace else.

"Yes . . . the appeal," one of them said.

"Let's clear the room and we can — "

"Excuse me!" called out the reporter as she pushed her way into the room, cutting off the mayor.

"I'm afraid this is a closed meeting!" the mayor said. "You'll have to leave, Ms. Parris."

"And I'm afraid I can't do that," she replied. "I was told – by you, in fact, Your Honor – that I had free range to go anywhere and film anything during the entire tournament. Did you not say that?"

"Well . . . I may have said that, but — "

"Before you go on with your statement," Ms. Parris interrupted, "let me get the camera rolling. I want to be able to show this response to the original guarantee you gave me, which is also on film."

The mayor looked like he'd suddenly swallowed his tongue. He repeatedly opened and closed his mouth but no words were spoken. The bright lights of the camera were switched on and aimed at him. He continued to try to speak, but the only things he could produce were beads of sweat rolling off his forehead.

"Please continue," Ms. Parris said.

"I . . . just think that . . . perhaps . . ."

"So I'm assuming that you have no further objections to my staying and witnessing the proceedings?" Ms. Parris asked.

The mayor nodded his head.

"Excellent!" she beamed.

The mayor turned to Coach. "It would have been better if you hadn't invited her along."

"I didn't invite anybody along except my team."

"And do you think that that is wise?" asked another one of the officials. "Having your players here?"

"It's about them, so why shouldn't they be here?" my father said.

"We're not going anywhere!" Kia said, stepping forward.

"Fine . . . fine . . . then please," the mayor said, "could you explain on what basis you are appealing our ruling that your player is ineligible to play?"

"On the basis that it's wrong," Coach said.

"There's nothing wrong about it," he replied. "This is the *Boys'* International Invitational Tournament."

"Not on any of the material that I received. Not on the application or brochures or your website information or the hand-outs you gave us when we registered."

"But it is officially listed in our founding charter as a boys' tournament," he argued.

"And as such, your player, being a girl, is not eligible to participate in this tournament," added one of the other officials.

"Then why didn't somebody mention that earlier? Like when I registered and included her birth certificate, which listed her as female, or at the reception, when I not only introduced her, but she was wearing a dress. Why wasn't it brought up then?"

It looked like none of the three men really wanted to deal with that one. Nobody stepped forward to offer an answer.

"I imagine you could say it was just an oversight," one of them finally answered.

"But one we did catch. And am I to understand that despite our ruling you chose to play your ineligible player?" questioned the third official.

"That's what my team decided, and I agreed with their decision one hundred percent!" Coach said.

"With that admission I'm afraid that we have no choice but to disqualify your entire team and — "

"Excuse me!" a voice piped in from behind me.

I turned around. It was the New York Wild Cats' coach. Coming in behind him was his team.

"Would anybody care to hear the opinion of another coach?" he asked. "The coach of the other team that's in the finals?"

Great, didn't he think that getting tossed out was enough? What did he want to do, kick us when we were down? Did they all need to crowd in here to gloat over us leaving?

"Certainly, Coach Barton, your opinion is always most welcome!" beamed the mayor.

"Thank you," he said as he walked to the front.

His team sauntered in. Most were still wearing their sunglasses. Those without shades looked at us like we were beneath them.

"I've been coming here for a long time now. My teams have been more successful than just about any team in the history of this tournament . . . as I'm sure you gentlemen are aware," Coach Barton said.

There was a nodding of heads from the officials. "In fact, if your team wins today you will become the winningest coach in the history of this tournament." the mayor added.

"*When* we win," one of his kids said under his breath.

"Yeah, *when* we win, not *if* we win," another added, and a teammate gave him a low-five.

"And the reason we keep coming back," their coach continued, "is because we have a chance to play against the very best teams."

"We certainly do our best to ensure that through the invitations," agreed one of the officials.

"So that's what's so confusing about this decision you've made," Coach Barton said. "You're on the verge of eliminating one of the top two teams in this tournament."

"Rules must be followed, Coach."

"You wouldn't think that if you'd just witnessed the game between this team and the Mumford team," Coach Barton said.

"Those refs were the worst," I said, much louder than I thought.

"I agree," Coach Barton said. "As I was saying, I brought my team here to play against the best. So before you make your final decision, I think you need to be aware that if you disqualify the Mississauga team, I will be pulling my team from the tournament."

"You can't be serious!" exclaimed the mayor.

"I'm serious. My team and I came to that de-